eden

ALSO BY JIM CRACE

JIM CRACE

eden

Regard the Angels and
their glisten'd Wings;
Behold their flightless underlings
At labour in the fields.
VISITATIONS 7:12

PICADOR

First published 2022 by Picador
an imprint of Pan Macmillan
The Smithson, 6 Briset Street, London EC1M 5NR
EU representative: Macmillan Publishers Ireland Ltd, 1st Floor,
The Liffey Trust Centre, 117–126 Sheriff Street Upper,
Dublin 1, D01 YC43
Associated companies throughout the world
www.panmacmillan.com

ISBN 978-1-5290-6243-4

1 3 5 7 9 8 6 4 2

A CIP catalogue record for this book is available from the British Library.

Typeset in Apollo by Jouve (UK), Milton Keynes
Printed and bound by CPI Group (UK) Ltd, Croydon, CR0 4YY

Visit **www.picador.com** to read more about all our books
and to buy them. You will also find features, author interviews and
news of any author events, and you can sign up for e-newsletters
so that you're always first to hear about our new releases.

1

THEIR ANGEL SUMMONS them. Three beak-strikes on the clapper of the orchard-bell mean that everyone nearby should set aside whatever tools they're working with or end their prayers at once and hurry to the trees where he is waiting with that oddity, a corpse. Of course, they have encountered death before, with shrews and beetles, say, with worms and moths, with fish. Small creatures without souls cannot expect, as can the garden's human habitants, to live eternally. But, still, a lifeless body is a jolt. It reminds the labourers what great fortunes they enjoy, fruitful and well-watered, if only they obey. They'll breathe forever without cares, they'll be provided for, they'll have no fears – if only they obey.

The body is a bird's, one of the many jacks that choose to gather in the nuttery's branching domes at dusk to air and share their grievances. Nobody counts the jacks as friends, but they are at least companions, during both labour and devotions. They mark the start and end of day with their self-proclaiming cries – jack-chat, jack-chat – protesting when the sun comes up, protesting when it sinks. But now it's just the middle of the afternoon in this high-growing corner of the lord's estate and, as instructed by the angel in his tousled blue plumage, the gardeners stare down at the body of the jack and decide which one it is specifically, which malcontent. Isn't this the bird whose wing never sat quite flat against its side but elbowed out, a gawky branch? They've noticed it was snagged and damaged, but how and where that damage came about they do not know.

How could they know? Like every flying creature in their realm – excepting angels, and probably the wrens, which are the garden's timid stop-at-homes – it must have ranged beyond the walls into the world, with all its perilous varieties, too many times not to have discovered the habits of caution. Out there, a jack has many things to fear: the boys, their sticks, their catapults, the falcon and the hawk, netting traps and glue snares, poisoned bait, all sorts of cats, the cooking pot, the ticks and lice and feather mites that plague most birds, a drought, a fire, a pestilence, the arrow and the spear, weasels with their appetites for eggs or chicks, feather hunters, snakes. What is there not to fear out there? But often, in the orchard, in the age-protected shelter of their trees, the gardeners have noticed this one many times, burdened by its injury, clumsy to the view, and so unlike its neat and jaunty brethren. Unhappy jack, they think as they stoop closer to its corpse. It was too briefly cursed with life. How death has whitened its eyes. Just yesterday they were as quick and silver as a snake's. Flies have already settled at its bloody beak. There is movement only in its feathers, which lift with the breeze, not greatly different from the feathers on the living angels' wings, listless when they're not reflecting light.

There is an angel they know – he oversees the stock pond, chirping out his orders to the fish – whose heart-side wing is damaged to the same degree as the jack's. He's a malcontent as well, though more so than any bird could ever be. That injured wing is punishment, he under-stands, for disobedience, for taking flight, for straying where he shouldn't stray, beyond the girdle of their enclo-sures to where dwell those outcast vassals of the earth whose lives are fleeting. He meant simply to test the air and satisfy a yearning to encounter for himself – though from on high, the bird's-eye view – their sorrows and their cares. It was to be the briefest of visits, in all inno-cence, and he always intended to observe the rules by keeping high and out of sight beyond the clouds. The lord instructs that angels are not to be seen by mortal eyes. At most they should appear as distant shimmers in the firmament, a mystifying flash of blue in blue. But the stock-pond angel was too beguiled by the busy world, the teeming to and fro outside of eden's holy bounds. He was lured so low by curiosity that he almost became – like any fruit bat, any swift – too hefty for his span. And he forgot his weight, his width, his lack of practice in the air. He'd spent too many lazy days with fish.

So, before he had a chance to witness anything or anyone close up, he snagged a wing on unkempt branches which stretched beyond the walls. If it can happen to a jack, it can happen to any feathered cousins. Angels included. He should have rested on the ground and caught his breath. But any master landing out of eden, just touching unblessed ground even for an instant, has sinned beyond the lord's forgiveness. He laboured heavily to stay aloft and damaged himself a second time, in his attempts to retreat across the battlement. The wing that tangled in the branches struck the holy masonry as well. He fears his clumsiness has damaged him beyond repair. Beyond salvation too. He struggles if he ever needs to fly within the garden. He's heavier than air – this broken angel called Jamin – and even when he is aloft, he is a quail rather than a lark. His flights are slow and arduous and comic to behold. Certainly, he no longer has the body to be a distant shimmering of blue in blue, let alone to gain the arch of heaven. Nowadays, he is hardly any value to the lord who, as everybody knows full well, did not create his angels to be earthbound or fashioned out of clay like men. The stories say they are the airborne outcome of an eagle and a dove, both magisterial and modest, powerful and meek, soaring and domestic, forbidding and forbearing, communal and divine. The lord has made them in the image of a bird, so that he can command them

4

to do anything by flight, so that the sky and what's beyond the sky is water to their wings just as the volumes and the currents in the stock pond are wind and air for fish. A creature that can penetrate the sky can serve his lord and his masters anywhere.

Nevertheless, it is, at times, a curse to be an angel, those labourers must think, for, even if an angel's wings are trim and have dominion in the skies, they are a hindrance on the ground. No wonder angels have so often prayed for hands instead of feathers. They conceal themselves to pray, closing their wing-tips level with their beaks and cloaking their ingratitude in the very plumes from which they are pleading for release. They have been refused, as yet. The lord allows four limbs – no more – for angels. He has allowed the same for birds and all the warmer beasts. Six limbs have been allotted for his beetles, wasps and ants. Eight are for spiders, scorpions and ticks, a copious allowance. Excessive, possibly. It's no surprise there are no limbs to spare for worms and snakes or for those creatures that are composed of light and smell and vapour. The gathered congregation at the jack's dull corpse are thankful they were not called upon to serve eternity as worms and snakes, and also glad not to be angels, despite the skies being out of reach for them, despite the distances to heaven. No, given any choice, they'd say that hands and arms are preferable to wings. Two thumbs are better than a beak. There are days, though, when – just as angels want for nimbler limbs – those unfeathered toilers in the gardens and the glebes would be grateful if the air could thin for them — not so that they could float above the earth or even fly but rather that their labours might be easier, their burdens weigh a little less, their shoulders, feet and fingers not ache so unforgivingly at night. Their never-ending lives are never-easing too.

See here, their angel tells the gardeners. His sentences are short when he is bringing messages. He is brisk and dutiful. Angels are not gifted in their speech. They're taciturn and best at giving orders or making their annunciations or providing sermons by rote. Two words — See here — suffice. His listeners will be reminded of the lesson of the jack, that this is what awaits them if they attempt what Adam did, and Eve, those countless times ago, and disrespect the congregation rules, only then to be expelled beyond the wall enclosing their broad gardens. That tainted couple took their shame into the world and died, as everybody out there must. What fools they were to sacrifice their lives for liberty. Their mouths were bloody and their eyes went white, just like this bird's. Flies and fleas settled on their wounds too.

The group of gardeners nod their heads a little wearily. They know this story all too well. They also mean to acknowledge the fresher warning he is giving them. Their angel is referring to what occurred just days ago and fears might happen again if this fever is allowed to spread, this vaunting curiosity and dangerous desire, this thirst for novelty. A sister from the orchard, a friend and companion everyone has worked, eaten, prayed and slept alongside for seasons beyond count, has disappeared and left her fellows puzzled and uneasy. Unless she is hiding like an animal in some dark hollow of the lord's estate, she must have made a passage through the undergrowth and violated the sacred rampart or else devised a secret channel of her own to take her from this blessed life to one that's doomed. By some reports – there are no witnesses, just hearsays – she connived to pass unnoticed through the great timber gates at the barbican, though they are opened only briefly once a week for alms and, every now and then, for oiling. By others, she squeezed through badger tunnels, blindly, underground. Rumour says there are a dozen ways of getting out, at least for anyone as spirited as her or anyone who is foolhardy enough to breech the limits of the lord. They call her Tabi – a tribute to her watchfulness and restiveness, a tabitha, a deer, though there is nothing doe-like in her boldness. She wanted to discover for herself, she's often said, cloaked and hidden by the night but talking to the darkness round her bed and to any sleepless ears. Discover what else there is other than eden's sublime uniformity. Find out what happens on the far side of the high, forbidden wall. Be elsewhere and beyond. Be out of bounds. Be gone, if only for a day. A single day of that seemed to her so much more tantalizing and extravagant than the everlasting days of this, the boredom and the certainty, those orchards laden year on year with their unfailing fruits, everything repeated and familiar, the domesticity, the blameless life she is ordained to lead.

Well, all of them must think the same, once in a while, no matter if they labour in the trees, as Tabi did, or stoop amongst the vegetables, or plough, or gather timber for the fire-women or the carpenters, or spin or weave or sew, or test their elbows kneading bread, or are one of those unlucky dykers whose job it is to irrigate the fields. Certainly, when it's their turn to endure the stinking task of slopping out the jordans and sluicing the latrines, they are allowed to hope for a better, sweeter, freer time, even if it is not endless or divine. Not one of them can say they've never dreamed of breaking out. Nobody dreams of always staying put, despite the perils and the torments of beyond. In bed at night, each of them is brave. The darkness is emboldening. But, in the light of day, they are as unlikely to try to cross the garden's wall into the world as they are to burst out of their own skins. Only Tabi is the sort to test her daring. She certainly has not stayed put. She's not been seen since they most recently ate fish, three evenings ago. Jamin was the last to spend much time with her. She has so often been his helpmate, feeding him and grooming him. That woman's underneath his wing in more ways than bear thinking of, they joke. He says she was her normal restless, joyful self, though when he speaks of her he cannot help but close his body off with wings. He is ashamed of something or has a secret and must hide himself.

The gardeners cannot help but share his shame. They too have secrets they should hide. They dare not let their angel sense their jealousy or see how low and anxious they've become since Tabi vanished from their lives, and how vulnerable. In their shaped and patterned world, any upset is unnerving. But Tabi's lonely exodus has been a blow. They feel unbalanced and unlaced, unravelled and exposed.

Their angel turns the jack with his taloned foot so that the group can clearly see the thoroughness of death, how it leaves nothing other than a shape, a weight, and then not even shape or weight when time has done its work. That bird will be as light and limbless as a stain or smell. Here, says the angel. You bury it. He is addressing a man known, for the gleaming darkness of his hair, as Ebon, though any of them there could just as easily turn over a wedge of soil at the edge of the nuttery and bury the corpse so it is out of sight and given back to the worms and grubs on which it has feasted for so long. But Ebon understands why he is chosen for this task. The angel knows that he and Tabi were tenacious friends, as close and intimate as doves. He has noticed, as has everybody else, how the man's shoulders have sagged of late and how his smile is no longer as ready as it was. It cannot be a secret that Ebon sorely misses her, despite the custom – it's a ruling, actually – that affections in the garden should be rationed equally, as must their food and water. Their beds were neighbours in the dormitory, they nearly always managed to pray and sing adjacently, and they spent their days together in the orchard and the nuttery, companions of the fruit. They shared the honour of that calling with pride. And so, of all the congregation, Tabi is – she was – the one whom Ebon cherishes the most. The angel does not doubt that if the woman's mutinous contagion could leave its smudge on anyone, Ebon is the likeliest. That's why he is the one required to bend and lift the body of the bird, to feel its hollow weight across his hands, and then to bury it. He'll get as close as anybody can in that eternal and protected place to death. He'll be less tempted to break out, once he has the body on his palm.

The jack is still warm to the touch, though that is mostly owing to the sun, which today has cleared the sky of any clouds and is providing what is called a ripener, or harvest heat. Ebon spreads his hands and lets the dead bird nestle there so that his brothers and his sisters can inspect the body closely, nose to feather, that's to say, or eye to bone. It's rare for them to get this near to animals. It's more than black, they realize; close up, its crown and wings are glossed with green and blue, its cheeks and nape are silvery.

The angel opens out his wings, displaying the briefest crossfigill, and goes, a bird in everything but name. A stormy rush of air, that's all. He has other tasks, further orders to impart, greater rulings to impose, and it is – in truth – uncomfortable for him to see the jack's feathered cadaver. His blue becomes just a glimmer in the corner of their eyes. A trace of breast down, not quite as heavy as the air, takes its time to reach the ground.

The gardeners blow the feathers of the corpse or touch the body with their fingertips. O, such an opportunity, beautiful and troubling, to be so close to the ashen, bloodless agonies from which they are themselves immune. They shake and nod their heads at death's dull and distant mystery, beyond experience. They are a little thrilled by it. They take their turns and take their time. They gather round and reach and stroke, and smell their hands. And then they touch again, to make quite sure the heart has truly stopped. Theirs, they know, might pump unceasingly but perhaps a little faster and less steadily at such a time as this, in their uneasy mood. A cherished sister's disappeared and that's the worst thing that's occurred in memory. And now this body of a bird. Misfortune often comes in threes, in legends anyway. Can they expect a third upheaval in their unvaried lives? They've heard the double boom of thunder. When will the lightning strike?

Ebon does his best to keep a steady hand and steady face for them, but, once he is alone again, he cannot stop himself imagining he is holding Tabi across his palms, that she is weightless, fading too, that somewhere on the far side of the barriers and palisades her body has begun to age and weaken, her time already ebbing out, that all too soon a slice of wormy soil will cover her. His stomach feels as tight as a wet knot, just from the thought of her.

He even speaks her name out loud. He cocks his head to pay attention to the afternoon. He half expects to hear her voice. Her calling back. Her coming home. But all he notices, other than the normal chatter of the trees, is the unwelcome squeak of a barrow's wooden wheel.

He buries the jack amongst the rotting apples that he and Tabi have raked up over the season into a sweet and sweating pile at the loamy end of the orchard and the nuttery. He has only to push the fruit aside with his foot to form a hollow, as soft and warm as any bed and just as full of bugs, and then to dig a little deeper with his spade. The smell is mellow, reasty, old. The jack has pecked at windfalls all its life and now is swallowed up in turn. It's right to give the body to the earth, to let it rot and liquefy along with fallen fruit. The jack's become a grubby feast for those with more limbs than the rest of us, and with none.

Rest well, Ebon says. He has covered the spading scar with windfalls. He knows he should say more, but there'll be prayers enough this evening. A death amongst the animals is nearly always marked with sermons – Let that little body be a warning to you all – so long as the departed creature's known to the congregation, as this jack is, or sweet enough, or simply gaily coloured and so lends itself to mourning. They're bound to be reminded too, by some bright and fretting angel, how fortunate they are not to be either birds or beasts but everlasting habitants of paradise. For the time being, though, Ebon only shuckles silent verses with his shoulders and his chin, then lifts his head, as everybody does each day once work is done, to wonder at the far-flung, mortal distance of the sky. His jack has flown into it, beyond the garden, countless times in its short life. Even its footprints have been arrows to the outside world. That's whence its bloody end derived. It takes only a moment and a toe, the warning goes, and death will sink its teeth into your foot, and death will syphon the blood from your veins, to satisfy its phantoms and its ghosts.

Yet Ebon almost relishes the thought of feeling death's sharp teeth sink in, because Tabi must have relished it as well. The more he can be like her, the closer he will be to her, he thinks, wherever that might be, no matter how she's suffering, whatever is in store. No, no, he can't imagine it. That world beyond the wall's a blank to him, a gap, a hollowness; thin air and idle dreams. He shakes his head but still the truth remains. The sister he has loved the most has departed for an empty space, a measureless chasm. She's transitory now. Time is already paling her. If he could press his hand onto her breast, he thinks, he might not even feel a heart.

The only certainty is this: his loss, her absence, has left Ebon as dry and brittle as a blown egg. He will condemn her sudden flight, if asked, and he has prayed already, many times, for her return and the lord's forgiveness for her trespasses. She has transgressed. There's no denying that. But Ebon cannot help but be as much in

13

awe of the risks she has taken as he is fearful of them for himself. He envies her for that. How bold a woman she has proved to be. What utter recklessness, to force gates, to scale a sacred and forbidden wall, to tunnel underneath the ground. He wonders if he can ever be that bold himself, unwise enough, to dip his toe just once, like her, to test the danger and the pain, to glean the orchards of the finite world, and know the difference, to see its towers and its roofs, to tell its beacons and its chimney pots, to witness people on the ground pursuing their short lives. The most that Ebon has ever seen from his rooted legs, or even from the branches of the trees he tends, are high and skybound marks of life beyond the gardens, the odd and lonely heavy swan, its shoulders set against the wind, the flocking residents of roosts and rookeries, the scarves of starlings and the ducking flights of wheezers, taking such delight in dusk. And he has seen as well the distant smoke of fires and heard the sound of bells and even caught the faintest chatter of the far-flung world when voices have been lifted by the wind and carried in, along with airborne seeds and feathers. The moon, the sun, the stars, of course; the moon, the sun, the stars that everybody shares, no matter where they are. But everything he knows about the outside world is airborne or celestial. He has never seen that solid ground that takes your life for only stepping on it lightly, for only pressing in a toe.

In these closing moments of the afternoon, standing in

the apple pile, the buried jack beneath his toes, his head thrown back to look freely at the dimming sky, Ebon finds himself more restless than he's ever been before. The death of birds, his missing woman, his snapped and wounded heart, the sheer and endless distance of the firmaments, are shaking him. They're prodding him between the shoulder blades. Go forward, Ebon. Go up to the garden's barbican and test your strength against the gates. Step out. It takes only a moment and – remember – just a toe, and then you'll be as free as she is free, for being free to die is also surely being free to live as well. He makes a promise there and then. He will be bolder. He'll see if he can summon up the sap to slip away and follow her. He has an image of them working side by side again, loading baskets with garden fruit, but where that garden is, in time or out of it, he cannot tell and does not, for the moment, want to care.

Now their angel summons them once more, though distantly this time and with the clapper on the kitchen bell. Six strikes. It's time for darkness to descend, for bats and stars, for singing, supper, prayers and sleep. Rest well, he says again. It's for the jack, the fruiting trees and for himself; it's for the woman who's lost to him, her dying day that ends again, and ends again, and ends.

2

SO THIS AWKWARD and unnerving day subsides, although briefly on a calmer note. The masters can't have helped but smell the unease in the air – for everyone, not just the orchardman – since Tabi disappeared. The ground beneath even the angels' feet has quaked with the shock and disrespect of her departure and the fear of having to explain it all to the garden's lord when they next dare to visit him. They understand their workers, now fewer than fifty, are bereaved and must be reassured at once, before the imp of disobedience takes hold like some fast-growing tare; and first one, then another, then a crowd grow bold enough to think that, possibly, the world is more enticing than eternity. Then what of eden? Those tares will multiply. Those fields and gardens will grow wild. The masters cannot tend them on their own. Those walls and barns and sacred roosts will age and crack like trees, weighed down by ivy, moss and vines, brought down by wind and time. And what of angels? Where will they take wing?

The order is sent, therefore, that once they have eaten, the gardeners must walk beyond the dormitory and the vegetable cloisters into the holier pavilions, a privilege more usually reserved for solstices and festivals, though, sometimes, for a lecture and a knuckle-rapping. That they are ill at ease is evident in how they walk. They go in single file, and, instead of striding shoulder to shoulder as they would between the gardens, they take measured and respectful steps. Their hands are either clasped behind their backs or hanging at their sides, as limp as tassels on a coat. Their lips are pursed. Only their eyes are busy, looking out for clues to why it is that they have been summoned at this hour and on this day when normally they could be digesting and relaxing by their beds. They are expecting chastenings – and cautions. They are expecting to be uncomfortable. It's all to do with Tabi, that's for sure. Their eden's felt untethered since she left. How fragile and how brittle they have all become.

Nobody likes these high and holy chambers. Their ceilings are too distant from the floor and too draped in darkness. The eaves and rafters are not even visible. And these rooms are never welcoming but damp and hushed and cheerless. There is, though, still light enough squeezing through the slender casements for everyone to see and pick a place on the thinly cushioned benches. They mill around. Nobody wants to be the first to sit and therefore lose control of who is sitting next to them. They have their daily favourites and their foes. But mostly they'd prefer not to have Ebon at their side on this rare occasion. It's only when he selects a place in the centre of the middle row that everyone else feels free to settle down. There's hardly room enough for all of them but still the orchardman ends up alone, an empty space on either side. That's where Tabi would have sat, in one of those two places, they tell themselves. They wouldn't want to take her space. They know that Ebon's crippled by her loss, so leaving him to sit alone is to offer him respect. But actually their choosiness this evening has more to do with fear. If Tabi's disappearance is indeed the reason why they've been so sombrely convened, staying away from her orchard-brother is only sensible.

The two gaps on the bench and their cold-shouldered orchardman are what the chosen angel first notices when he enters from his loft. The spaces almost make Tabi seem more present than if she were sitting there in the flesh. He cannot help but nod and smile to himself. He will not even need to mention her name. His warnings can be subtle, undeclared almost. His audience have clearly understood his purposes and what they should expect. All that is required of them for now is silence and still-ness while he preaches in his high-fluted and consoling voice. The only movement ought to be from candle flames, bucking slightly in the draughts. Their scent is lemon balm and lavender – that is the angels' choice, for it disguises the day's end smell of labourers. It also masks the musky niff of feathers.

There should be no need this evening, after the rich harvest we've enjoyed this season, to remind you of your blessings and how lucky you have been to be created servants of the lord, the master instructs, repeating what he has been told to say by his more priestly brethren. Instead let's make a list of your misfortunes. Please have the confidence to stand and speak. The lord allows you to be meek but also wants you to be bold, when asked.

Now all but one lift their heads and show surprise. This is not something they have heard before. Nor are they used to such an invitation. To stand and speak, indeed. To offer their complaints. There is an excited silence as the habitants of eden, made sluggish by the heavy meal they've just enjoyed and by the failing light, the silence and the candle scents, perk up and twist around to see which of them responds while certain it will never be themselves. Most eyes have rested on Ebon. Amongst them all he is the one most likely at the moment to be so beset by doubts he cannot hold his tongue. He has misfortunes, certainly. But he sits still, much stiller than they can themselves, they think, as if he means to be as silent and unfeeling as the chamber's marble tiles. His hands are trapped between his knees. His head is bent. The candlelight is gleaming off his hair.

It's then that everybody hears the scuffing from

above, though no one dares to tilt their eyes and peer into the darkness overhead. But they don't need to look any further than the floor to know that what they've heard is real. Whatever's scuffing has dislodged a shower of dust and timber smut which has descended in a glinting column to settle almost at their feet. One of the candles briefly flares. The angel sees and hears it too. There's someone, something, shifting on the rafters out of sight and billowing the air. It weighs enough to make the timbers wheeze. No bat or pigeon is that large. The lord is, though. They've been told countless times in sermons and in homilies that, on the days of judgement, he will descend from his high palaces to sit with them and list their sins and draw an end to time. And then the never-ending days will radiate as everlasting stars. The seasons will be moons and suns. All breathing souls will turn to dust, just like the dust that's falling on them and the candles now. Until those days, the lord will be forever watching, from on high, the habitants of his estate. So nothing they might do or say amongst themselves can remain unknown to him.

Some fine story, Tabi's often said. The masters' master is nothing more than hearsay. But creaking rafters can't be argued with, nor can the heavy certainty, felt by everybody in the chamber, that they are being scrutinized. The lord is maybe only checking that they are attentive while the angel speaks. Or listening for grievances and mutiny. Or testing who's been fool enough this evening to knock knees and elbows with Ebon. But certainly – whatever Tabi says or thinks – he's close. The lord is on a rafter overhead and judging them. There's not a person now who shares in Ebon's muttered prayers that the creaking timbers and the billowing are evidence that Tabi's tucked away up there, but nor is there a single one who doesn't copy what he is already doing. That's to say: they trap their hands between their thighs, they bow their heads towards the candlelight and sit as still as stone. Certainly, no one is fool enough to list misfortunes in the presence of the lord.

So nothing, then? the angel asks eventually, though now his voice has become more anxious and more stilted. He's almost sure who's in the rafters, wrapped in the darkness. It will be one of the priestly angels, checking up on him and everything he says, seeing that he does not deviate but preaches reverentially. He's nervous now and starts to shift from foot to foot. He spreads his wings with all the drama he can muster as if he means to hug everybody to his chest but in doing so fans out a couple of the flames. Their wicks briefly wink and glow, then twist with smoke, then die. The shadows in the corners of the pavilion stretch closer to the congregation, enfolding them. It's hard to tell one person from another now. May I enquire, the angel continues, but more quietly than before, hoping to recover from what has been his clumsiness, are you like candles, short of life and easy to put out? Like jacks, indeed. That life of squawks and squabbles is brief and brutal, isn't it? As some of you have seen today. Does anybody here feel hunger like a jack? Please lift a hand if you have less to eat than is seemly and appropriate. Are you cold at night and have no pillow for your head? Is anybody here unloved? Unwell? Afraid? Do you enjoy the consolations of community? Is anybody here alone? He looks directly at Ebon's head, almost daring him to speak. Are you required to take care of these grounds without a hat upon your head or shoes upon your feet? Still nothing? Then let us sit in silence and contemplate – with thanks – what eden gives to us.

And so they do. They sit upon their damp and cushioned benches in that sweet-smelling room in the shallows of that balmy evening at the end of harvest time, and contemplate the comforts they enjoy, and have enjoyed, and will enjoy for ever and a day unless they're fool enough to try what Tabi's evidently done and Ebon might, and turn their backs on paradise.

But once they're in the open air again and heading through the moonlit cloisters to their beds, there's not one amongst the habitants who doesn't draw deep breaths and wonder what those restless rafters heavy with the lord might signify and what his falling dust might mean for them. They sniff the air and what they smell is mayhem, tumult, danger, change.

3

ALUM WILL BE the only habitant to not attend the angel's
sermon in the candlelit pavilion. He'll have other duties
to perform and his own anxieties. It is his public, daily
task to stock the larder for their communal meals. He carries produce – freshly lifted, cut or picked – from the
vegetable beds, the orchards, the granges and the meadows
to the kitchens. He ought to be more welcomed and more
loved. His is an easy occupation, restful and unsuper-
vised, and his reward for being useful to the lord's estate.
For this he has fashioned himself a barrow out of oak and
a deep, spale trug with a rim and an arched handle made
from hazel wands. He is no craftsman. They're rough-
hewn. The knots are dry; the laths warped and gaped
within a season of their making. The wood is splintered
at the handle's curve. The barrow's wheel is noisy and
untrue. It squeaks a warning: Alum's on his way, Beware,
beware, Pretend he isn't even there. But he is proud of

his handiworks, and defensive, even of the squeak. They are the trappings of high status, he believes. They are his regalia and his company. It isn't wise even to touch them, let alone reach in for something ripe and tempting when his back is turned. True order has to be observed or there is lawlessness, he'll say. Obedience is harmony.

A day or so before she went missing, Alum caught Tabi leaning over his barrow with her fingers round the fruits of a newly cut tomato vine. Just plumping them, she claimed, but there were juices on her lips, and lies. He could not stop himself from wiping the back of his hand across her mouth, to rob her of the flavour. Still she clutched on to the vine. He had to bend her fingers back until they almost snapped before he could persuade her to let go. Anybody else would have let go at once, for fear of worse. Alum has the garden's sharpest knife with which to harvest fruit and squashes and a long-handled trowel for the roots and tubers. He might well use them on a scrumper or a pick-pear, given half a chance. Certainly, he can be bruising with his fists. Ask anyone.

He is also the angels' go-between, their hither and their thither, and that – more than his bruising ways – is why he is not loved and cannot truly like himself. He carries evidence and chatter to the superior angels – not to Jamin, that one's disloyal, as Alum knows too well and has reported it; nor to any of the lesser-winged task-masters whose only purpose is to light and guard, to rule

24

and guide the workers and the gardeners, and be waited on – but to the five or six angels, the archest and most priestly ones, who are themselves the greater go-betweens, who speak and listen to the lord. In his time he has observed habitants concealing food, or spoiling work completed by another, or beating their tough hands against a tabletop or the trunk of a tree to vent their anger at some petty slight or inconvenience. He's seen his fellows hurt themselves, even tugging at their own hair so forcibly that blood is drawn, or – once – taking red-hot embers from the fire and holding them between three fingertips just for the ecstasy and oddity of having scars. He's caught people sleeping during prayer, faking illnesses when they're fit, stopping work before the bell, taking short cuts like a fox instead of sticking to the designated paths. If Alum ever doubts his usefulness, it is incidents like those – conveyed to the angels, while both the blood and embers of the offences are still warm – that can persuade him what he does is honourable, while what he witnesses and then reports is rarely so. Anything beyond the pale is worth the telling in his view. The proudest boast for Alum – other than his trug and his barrow – is that his reports might wing up to the heavens, that his name is known and mentioned there. What higher purpose or what greater honour can there be?

Alum's severity and his impatience, he tells himself more than once a day, is in the service of the lord and, therefore – though they might not acknowledge it – in the interests of everyone who dwells beneath the canopy and so is blessed with everlasting life and with the garden's never-ending benefits. He's sacrificed his local popularity, perhaps, by how he earns his crust and by the unforgiving way he employs his thorny eyes and even sharper tongue. That is the hard and bitter truth. Yet that is how he daily proves his loyalty and diligence to the winged nobility. They, surely, are the only ones that count. An angel matters more than any labourer.

It is a fiercely lonely life. Alum might never be hugged or kissed as others are. There are times – such as the harvest feast or the solstice revels – when grievances are normally set aside, but still he is not trusted or embraced but is regarded as the banquet's skull, to be at best ignored. At mealtimes, he has grown used to sitting like a stranger at the table, sharing no one's bread and rubbing no one's thighs. If he shifts along the bench to help himself to salt or spice or water and to better overhear the talk, all chatter ends and his fellows finish up and hurry off to sleep. Then silence falls as soon as his broad face is spotted in the dormitory. His bed, he notices, is often pushed a little closer to the wall and further from his neighbour's than when he left it in the morning. Nobody wants to share with him the air they breathe communally, it seems, even when they're dreaming. The man can spot temptation in their souls before they've even fantasized the sin.

So, in the mornings, if he chooses, he can sit with his back to all his brothers and sisters while he pulls on his boots and burrows into his clothes. He does not have to meet their eyes or hope to join in any chatter. He prefers it that way – or so he tells himself – despite the solitude, for if he faces them, they might turn away. Besides, although his back is turned, his ears are pricked and finely tuned. Everyone is careful of what they say and what they do. For fear of being caught by him. For fear of being in his debt. And those that lapse? Perhaps there is no need to bother angels with a report of this, he'll say. In return, he might expect some gratitude. He'll let them know, when the need arises, what form their gratitude should take. No good will come of breaking rules or breaking free, except the benefits that come to him. No wonder they avoid him when they can.

But Alum is hardened to their lack of friendliness. It is the price he has to pay. Their iciness is understandable. It's envy. He's closer to the angels than any of them can ever hope to be. It is as if he's sprouted wings himself. No, what he wants – demands, in fact – is not false warmth from his so-called equals but deference. If the angels will not tolerate disrespect, nor should he. He's asked them for permission to judge and punish any insult, any lack of due regard, that's offered him. He'd like, if only they'd allow it, a fenced-off corner of some barn to be his prison-house. A hungry day or two of darkness and damp straw would surely cure anyone of disrespect. A sister could be shut in there for stealing from his trug, he suggests. There'd be no call to let her go until she prayed – until she wept, indeed – for the lord's mercy. A brother could be locked away for sleeping too late. Or gluttony. Or being careless in his speech. But, no, you're not the one to judge, he has been told countless times by his masters, but just the one to see and tell: load your barrow with any secrets and deceits or any spoken discontents that are produced amongst your siblings and bring them here to us.

For this, he does not carry any tools. He does not need a sickle or a spade. All he needs are ears and eyes, a nose for gripes and grievances, the trick of reading people's minds and a talent – so he thinks – for being treacherous without always seeming so. He counts himself as upright and dependable, given half a chance. Memories are short in gardens without time; he understands and takes great comfort in the thought. What does it matter if each day he makes a new enemy and refreshes an old one? Forgiveness is forgetting.

This second occupation is less restful than his first. His work is never finished, even when – as now, in the embers of the afternoon – he's out of mind and out of sight on his last kitchen task, foraging for cobs and filberts in the orchard's furthest corners for the morning's breakfast bowls. There is a huge and glossy walnut that he likes. Its broad-domed crown produces such a shade that anybody standing in it might seem almost to disappear. It is a casual, calming place where Alum has often spent an afternoon of planning, stretched out on a mattress of leaf mould and loam.

Alum wheels his barrow there, expecting only the company of beasts and birds at that time of the afternoon, but it is soon clear he does not have the orchard to himself after all. He hears a voice, not far away, calling out a name. It's Ebon's voice. It's Tabi's name. This is the moment when the damaged jack is being lowered to the ground and buried in the apple pile. Alum watches from afar, alert as ever, but not quite understanding what he sees or hears. He does not know this is a funeral, for Ebon has the body almost hidden in his hands. Its shape is hardly visible.

The orchardman turns towards the downing sun to see how much day – and how much work – remains and what time he'll have to spare for this small burial. Beyond the birdsong, the tippety-chip of distant tools, the countless sounds that trees are bound to make, he has already heard the telling squeak of Alum's barrow being pushed by the same hands that all too recently very nearly snapped Tabi's fingers. Ebon barely turns to look, but, even when the barrow is lowered and silenced, he can identify the shuffle of leaf litter and woodland duff and see Alum's moving shadow below the walnut's dark, concealing boughs. Ebon knows that he is being watched and he will take great care not to transgress in any way. It's understood by everyone that Alum is the angels' man and should be defied only by a fool. Or by a woman whose spirit, sometimes, is unwise. Yet he does not step across with greetings and the usual deferences, as might be required on any normal afternoon. The corpse is more important than the go-between.

For a moment, though, neither man can help but catch sight of the other and give themselves away. There's no pretending now. Still, they do not even nod or lift a hand to wave. You first, not me, their bodies say. Yet, having heard the grieving hollowness in Ebon's voice when he cried out his missing sister's name, Alum cannot fail to recognize, even from a distance, even in that briefest twinning of the eye, the look on the man's face and how forlorn it is, how sorrowful. The familiar, optimistic shine, which Alum cannot make himself admire as others do, has dulled on it or, at least, become less legible.

Alum smells a prey, and pauses for a moment. He's witnessed brothers and sisters dreaming of escape countless times before. They do their best to be expressionless and calm – to hide the flutter of their hearts, to keep their purposes disguised – but they succeed only in seeming guarded and furtive. Ebon is certainly looking unusually and unconvincingly solemn, Alum thinks. He's made his face a mask and masks are worn only as camouflage, and camouflage is there only to fool an onlooker. Alum knows these signs of restlessness, these seams of discontent. He's made a reputation out of knowing them. He is aware as well – too well aware, for it's a tricky problem that he must resolve – that the orchard-hand called Tabi, the one who's always been the duck to Ebon's drake, the one who was so thrillingly defiant with tomato on her lips, has somehow managed to escape into the world without the angels' go-between even smelling it.

Now Alum's nostrils flare to test the orchard air. The smell is nut and apple sweet. Quite innocent, perhaps. But apples were the smell of man's first disobedience, as everybody knows. What the angels' man detects this afternoon with his practised nose is further disobedience. He'll have to put a stop to that. Where he has failed with Tabi, he will succeed with her devoted drake. It is time, he decides, to show himself more openly and demand some courtesy. He will insist on being greeted. But, now that he is standing up and stepping out of the walnut's shelter, he notices the corpse in Ebon's hand. A bird. A jack. Ah, there is to be a burial. Even for a man like him, it isn't wise or kind to interrupt when death is being planted underground.

Alum backs away into the shadows of the orchard to observe from a greater distance this latest malcontent . . . or mourner; only time and snooping will determine which. The walnut shields him again. Disguised by dappled light and by the grey-green cloak he always wears, he watches Ebon fondling the jack's cold corpse. He witnesses the turning of the soil and senses other things are being turned as well.

It is not until the bird has been buried beneath its

mushy shroud of windfalls and Ebon has muttered his Rest Wells that Alum hears – far off – the supper bell. Six strikes of the clapper end the working day for all the labourers and gardeners. They have a chance to wash themselves and tidy up, or stretch their limbs and ease their backs, before candlelight, when they'll need to take their places in the dining room, for food and prayer and singing. It is normally an opportunity, as well – though it is brief – for any of the sisters or the brothers to idle by their beds or play their games of knap-and-clap, or simply please themselves in their own company. But tonight is different. They've all been summoned to attend a sermon in one of the holy rooms. Alum does not need to go. He still has work to do, and duties. He really must report at once to angels. They should be pleased with him.

4

THE BROKEN ANGEL called Jamin is not unhappy with his lot, despite the damage to his wing. Indeed, in many ways it is a blessing not to fly. He cannot for the moment even contemplate another wounding and reckless excursion across the wall, just to satisfy a yearning. Nor can he be called upon to carry messages above or even to display too stridently the power of his rank below. For the moment, he's a groundling too, though a helpless one. While he is still nursing his injury – long may it last, so long as there's no pain – the beck and call of daily life can pass him by. He counts his blessings, certainly. The lord's estate does not weigh heavily across his mantle or tug his wing-tips or his tail as it does so many of his betters. Instead, he spends the sunlit hours with his fish at the garden's stock pond, delivering commands as sweetly as he can to the pair of wingless helpmates whose job it is to keep the carp, the eels and spotted bellygills content and healthy. The fish are fed at dawn and dusk with kitchen waste and – cruelly – with earthworms or any sulphur-smelling brandlings that are rash enough to show their guts and ganglions on the surface of the soil or amongst the leaf litter. Sometimes Jamin picks these up himself, a momentary sparrow, and drops them from his beak into the stretching throat of some keen fish, but mostly he prefers to roost and watch from his raised angel bower, as peaceful and untroubled as a dove, nursing his ungainly limb, hoping to recover, though not too speedily, while others do the work. The fish and water keep him calm and kind, he thinks. He's no rebel, but is inclined to respect and admire – to be envious of, indeed – the greater angels, despite their evident disdain for him. They take him for a clumsy fool.

Jamin's assistants are requested to make sure that the water – rising unseen from holy springs – is netted and kept clean, that the surface is clear of dreg and scum, that the beds of bitter leaves and cress are tended lovingly and the blanket weed removed, that heron do not have the chance to land, that supper fish are netted from the pond each holy day and seventh day and taken flapping to the flapping cooks. Such work does not send anyone to bed at night with aching limbs or ringing ears, and that is why Jamin is popular. Everybody wants a chance to work for him and spend the best part of the day on easy tasks, and then to idle – short-term angels for the afternoon – doing nothing more strenuous than watching stock fish breaking surface with their backs or stooping down to examine their own rippled faces mirrored in the pond. It's restful there, and healing. So that's the reason that the work's reserved for any hands who are unwell or injured. Even those who do not age will suffer at some point in eternity from aches and pains and chills. Some of these hands are victims of the angels' Nose – his fists and feet, his trowel, his fingernails, his squeak. They nearly always finish up at Jamin's side, nursing their wounds on the banks and in the shallows of his pond. He hears their complaints, day upon day. He witnesses the hurt expressed across their faces. He sees their bruises colouring, and therefore, of all the angels, he's the one who least values Alum and his labours.

So it happens that Tabi – a day before she disappears – comes to Jamin's place to be his helpmate at the pond. She is not fit enough for orchard-work. She cannot safely swing an axe or climb ladders or undertake any of the tasks that she and Ebon have planned for the day, some hazel coppicing, some cutting out of barren wands and suckers, the gapping up of weaker trees, all jobs requiring energy and a good, firm grip. Her fingers on one hand are badly twisted. They are bruised and swollen and painful when she flexes them. She might have fractured one or two, she says, though – wisely – won't say how, not to an angel anyway. The tittle-tattle is that Alum's broken them. She's paying for tomatoes with her splintered bones. Alum was reminding her that there's a penalty for pilfering. What creature in the garden, though – including the most exalted – has not been tempted by the common fruit that grows in such abundance? Jamin himself, made peckish and impatient on a summer's afternoon, has often helped himself to food intended for the table. Indeed, he's taken from the snitch's beloved produce trug more than once or twice and never been discovered. Tabi has been unlucky to be caught, red-handed and red-lipped.

Jamin has always liked the orchard-woman, unruly though she is. He has admired her spirit, longed for her attentions, wanted to pass time in her capricious company, just to add a little of her sweet and bitter zest to what his fellow masters call the accidie of their angelic lives, the sloth, the boredom and ennui. What kind of benefice is theirs? So, when she arrives that morning, her forehead creased with pain, he suggests at once that, rather than labour amongst the fish and cress, she should rest with him and share his shade until both of her hands are truly fit for harder work. It will be a treat to have her at his side for one whole day at least. Perhaps there might be more if that bent hand is slow to heal. Besides, for reasons that are not entirely free from ill will or jealousy, he's eager to learn, fresh from the source, exactly how her fingers have been snapped. He hopes to hear her say the name of that one immortal who is more valued by the masters in the lofts than Jamin himself. He'll get her talking. He'll find out.

It's said – ordained, in fact – that angels cannot hate.

They are the guardians of love and harmony. Possibly, when they were first engendered by the lord on his fifth day and sent out to fly across the dome of the sky as his custodians and heralds, they might have been unblemished. But time . . . well, time erodes, especially when there is no end to it. Just as the immaculate and unageing bodies of the gardeners have nevertheless thickened and grown tough from their hard work, and their hands, once as clothy and as flexible as mullein leaves, have grown calluses and cankers, so the angels can't be blamed for hardening. Their unflagging duties of command, of control and discipline, do not nurture patience or charity but only ruffle feathers. So angels have become as likely as anyone else to suffer from a vice or two, to be imperfected by the never-ending weight of their impeccability. Pomposity and pride are the commonest of their failings, along with spite. Jamin is largely innocent in this regard. He's not generally judgemental of his flightless friends either, especially those immortals who are sent to share his working day. His loathing is reserved for only one. The go-between, of course. He was the man who surely must have spied on Jamin and told the greater brethren that this lowly angel's wing was damaged out of eden, above unholy ground, without permission for so low a flight, in contravention of the rules. How else could they have known about his clumsy yearning for the world and called him to their lofts for reprimands and warnings? Jazib, the greatest of them, said to him, Do not suppose

37

that angels cannot be expelled from here. Jamin would have to be as cool as stone not to be aggrieved by that, and not to want some retribution to swoop down, its talons unforgiving. Say what you want about the angels of the lord but they are not fashioned out of stone. Nor are they made, despite their claims, with only honey in their veins.

No, Jamin detests the go-between. It's not angelic, but he does. And he would like to see his fall from grace. He can imagine a not too distant day when the man, no longer anybody's eyes and ears, is just a common labourer, a digger in the mud, a beast of burden in the fields, a toiler in the moil, another pair of hands who'll work his bully fingers to the bone and have to spend a so-called day of rest and recovery at the stock pond under Jamin's command. O how the gentle angel will torment him then. How hard he'll make him work amongst the mud and weed. He'll have him clearing stones from the deepest parts. He'll have him picking out the duckweed with his fingertips. The go-between will be as damp and lowly as a worm. It is meanly satisfying to imagine him, dangling from a master's beak, as supper for the fish.

Tabi greets the angel, Jamin, as she would any friend and neighbour, pushing back his plumage with her one good hand and pressing her nose against his nape. A kiss? Almost a kiss, but dovelike and nuzzling. The feather and the lip have touched, despite the rules of conduct. She spends the day perched at the angel's side, watching the idling carp, the thrashing eels performing knots and clusters, the bellygills lurking in the belly of the pond and belching air. It is transfixing, just to see the water rippling and frowning as the breeze, the sunlight and the hidden spring combine their many textures and their patterns. Her morning passes like a dream. But later in the afternoon, when the pain has settled down a bit and she is tired of watching fish and bored by so much leisure, she's content to do what Jamin loves and groom his breast and wings and tail, as she's been called upon to do before.

An angel's feathers are similar to birds', despite their ostentation and flamboyance. No bird – no macaw, bunting or jay – can boast a blue as deep as Jamin's, though. Or any of his brethren's. Even the kingfisher is muted in comparison. Angels who have seen the sea, when they're aloft enough on cloud-free days and on their way to heaven, may recognize their own blazonry repeated in the sunlit waves below, but those colours of the ocean are fleeting and those patterns are temporal. A moment passes and the sapphire is slate, another moment and the slate is jade, and then the jade is silvery. An angel's blue, however, is everlasting. It's heavenly and deep. The only other blues that can compare with it are found in pastures in the spring – those vivid speedwells and cornflowers – or sometimes in a human eye. A blue-irised woman, such as Tabi, is said to have twin angels in her eyes.

It's just as well that Tabi likes the feel of feathers and understands their qualities. She knows she cannot simply bunch and ruffle them like she might a neighbour's hair, or Ebon's hair, as she has done so frequently and gladly. They are not soft and springy like a human mane but flat and fragile. Their tendency is rigid, head to tail. Still, it's comforting for her to stroke and smoothe them, respecting how they nap and shiver underneath her hand, how the colours duck and shine as they angle to the light, their gloss and matt, how the interlocking barbs can rearrange themselves in perfect plush no matter how severely they are split or parted. It is a satisfying craft to groom an angel perfectly.

She starts with Jamin's throat and nape, where the feathers are at their downiest and mostly there for show. He's sticky and encrusted on one side below his beak and amongst the lores around his eyes by the pips and juices he has dined upon, the pith and pulp of feeding. She smiles to herself when she discovers and removes tomato seeds. She only uses her undamaged hand – and is careful not to nudge his damaged wing – but digs her healthy fingers in to locate and scratch the flesh below the feathers and the down, hoping not to find too many pod-lice, ticks or mites, though knowing she is bound to find a few. The utter dryness and the warmth are always a surprise. No wonder angels keep away from fire. And no wonder they avoid the heavy knockabouts of daily life. An angel, underneath his finery, feels bony-thin and delicate.

Tabi never works against the vane but follows the shaft, a subtle hollow thing, towards the feather-tips, loosening whatever fluff there is and brushing out trapped particles of leaf and chaff. She reaches places that an angel cannot reach himself.

It isn't long before Jamin has ducked his head into his chest and is cooing, wheezing, bristling. His eyes are closed, his bill slightly parted, his crest aroused. She's put him in that place which is neither sleep nor ecstasy but is restful, sinful and distantly familiar. He feels the solace and the shame of taking comfort from her hands. Jamin half opens just a single eye and studies Tabi through the blurring screen of his cheek feathers. The pleasure she provides so willingly and teasingly is an eternity of sorts, he thinks, though it is spiced, he must suspect, with mockery. Her eyes are giveaways: she is amused by him rather than beguiled. So what? Each moment seems to never end and yet his heartbeats mark the galloping of time with countless finishes. He watches her as, surely, Ebon watches her, as everybody watches her, and even Alum watches her despite himself, with scorching, blushing tenderness. This isn't passion and it isn't love. No, such indulgences are only for those creatures of time and memory beyond the battlement. It is devotion, though, and certainly sublime. Jamin has to shake away the thought – both sacrilege and blessing – that right now he cares for Tabi and her fingertips more than he cares even for the lord.

She pushes her good fingers through his breast, sides and flanks repeatedly, building up a rhythm of strokes and massages until her wrist begins to ache and she needs to rest. He lifts his head and pushes his crown against her shoulder, nudging her for more, his eyes still closed. Be patient, she demands. And he is patient, waiting for her to recover and begin again. The woman's in command. He lifts his angel chin and bares his throat for her, a helpless supplicant.

Tabi flexes her wrist and chuckles to herself. Something old and mischievous has stirred in her while she was delving into the angel's plumage. What saps and fools they are, for all their blue and vibrant wings, for all their loftiness, dependent on inferiors. That is the purpose of an angel, Tabi thinks, his only role, to be served and waited on, fed and groomed by humankind. That's why the lord has made us everlasting, free from death, because the angels need us so. They can't caress themselves. Or build, or cook, or use a hoe, or scratch their backs, or make a barrow out of wood. Or grow tomatoes, come to that. An angel's good for nothing, except for ringing bells. And prayer. They cannot even clean themselves.

Again, Jamin opens just a single eye to watch her massaging the tendons in her wrist and causing evident pain to the injured hand in doing so. They flinch and wince in unison. So sister, Jamin says at last, how have you hurt your fingers? Tell me the story of your injury. What have

42

you done to warrant it? Confess it all. I'll not say any-thing to any of my brethren, or yours. I am, you know, the angel you can trust.

She will not answer him at once. She has a secret that is too dark to share. She means to punish eden for its hateful go-between – and abandon it. It can't be hard to climb that outer wall. Even if the stone is sacrosanct, it must still have toeholds. You'll miss us if you leave, the angels warn in every lesson they teach. You'll miss us in . . . unkind ways, too sudden to imagine. The word Unkind seems menacing. But she does not know what she might miss without first breaking free and missing it. She won't miss Alum, that's for sure.

She begins to work on him again, first combing her fingers through the nape and mantle on his upper back, then working down. It's only then that she finds her first plump tick, distended with the angel's blood. It's berry-black. The feathers there are working parts, not decorations. The quills and shafts are hard and durable. The barbs and vanes are tough and stringy. Tabi has to dig quite deep to get her fingers round the tick. She pulls the angel's feathers back until the blob of blood is vis-ible. She spits on it and, when it puckers and shrinks itself, she flicks it off and has it lying like an onyx bead in the middle of her palm. She stores it on her lap while she continues with her search, into the scapulars, the flanks, the rump, the coverts and finally the tail.

She's finished now. She's found four more. She gives

Jamin a final scratching of the throat, in his softest down, and then disposes of the ticks. She throws them high. The first one misses and lands too short. That tick will see another day, but the other four plop noisily into the closest reaches of the pond. The eels are quicker than the carp. The surface boils and then goes still again. There are ripples, then the slightest blush of blood, then nothing but reflections of the sky.

At last she answers him. The tell-tale caught me with a juicy mouth, she says.

BUT WHAT TABI cannot say or even admit to herself until she is in bed that night and tucked away in her own company at the close of what has only been a restful day is how chafed and nettled she is feeling generally. She is still angered by the go-between. While there is any pain remaining in her wrist and hand, she is bound to daydream her revenge on him. How she would love to toss and plop him like a tick into the pond, then watch the water boil again with blood. How she would like to be the wind that drops a piece of rotting timber on his head. How she would like to shove and sink him into the mire of the latrines. A busy, squatting man can't be hard to topple. But thinking ill of Alum is nothing new or rare. He isn't loved by anyone. Disliking him is something she has shared for many seasons now and, unless she gets away, she can look ahead to many seasons more of it. And there will be further injuries, no doubt. The man takes every chance to seize her by the wrist or neck or waist. He likes to mark her with a bruise. In some respects, she would not want him to be kinder, for sometimes it seems that both avoiding him and provoking him have become her only entertainment. Even the bruises are more exciting than unblemished skin. A bruise is just a memory made flesh – something meaningful that fades and mends.

What is new, though, and troubling is her growing irritation with everybody else, her brothers and her sisters who have never done or even wished her any harm but simply want her company and are amused by anything she says, no matter how uncivil. Nowadays she can hardly match the warmth of their bright greetings and their ready, placid smiles. She'd rather be alone, high in the branches of a tree, than have to take part yet again in conversations that she's had a thousand times before. She longs to be as startled by them as they are by her but never is. They might just as well be cooing doves, she thinks, as she fails to fall asleep that night. Indeed, the dormitory is sounding like a cote of roosting birds, docile and complacent: We're dreaming here. We're cooing here, hroo-hroo. We're only half alive. Amongst all her neighbours and companions in their forty or so mattressed beds – the bare-timbered two, long-since stripped, once belonged to Adam and to Eve, the garden's thrilling absentees – is she the only one astir? Is she the only one to be awake by day as well? Is she the only one whose blood runs fast at the prospect of another bed made bare?

She turns her back on most of her neighbours and stares into the greater darkness of the dormitory's far end where Alum sleeps, a step or two apart from everybody else. His breathing is mechanical and loud. Even her companion of the trees is deep in sleep though within reach. If she but stretches out an arm, she can touch his skin and hair and even feel his breath against her fingertips. She almost does so but draws back her hand before her fingers catch his face. If he were to wake, she would only vex him with anxieties, and he would only vex her with his peacemaking. Even Ebon is an irritant tonight. How can the man be so untroubled, so cheerfully reliable, so satisfied, when all the future offers him is repetitions of the past?

Count your blessings, one to five, she mutters to herself. That is what the angels advise their charges to do if ever they are waylaid by doubts or temptations. A troubled spirit never sleeps, they say. Slumber is for tranquil hearts. So Tabi brings her good hand up from underneath her blankets and presses the fleshy cushion of its heel against her mouth, as she's been taught, to recite her blessings and tap each of them out on her forehead, one finger at a time. Her palm smells strongly of the angel's feathers, an acrid souvenir of how she's spent her afternoon and how even Jamin in her current mood is also an annoyance and, for all his gentleness, no less helpless or demanding than any other of the masters. Grooming him is labour too. Everything is work.

She does her duty and totals the five blessings. Her thumb is witness to the love the lord bestows on her. Her pointing finger is the safety and the care provided by the angels. The middle finger stands for plenty, the riches of the table and the garden. The fourth is warmth and shelter. And the last, the little sapling of the five, is to know the joys of life eternal. What more can a person want than love and care, and those abundances of living which will never end with dying? They might want to know what other loves there are, besides the lord's, Tabi cannot help but think. And they might care to wonder what the perils are of stepping out from underneath the angels' wings. And they might choose to experience, for a day or two at least, a life without abundance, for scarcity gives value. As for everlasting life? Such a blessing – if it means anything at all – is beyond reach and meaning, always distant, always immaterial. The masters say it is the stream that never dries but pumps out an endless flow of days and months and years unceasingly. It is supposed to be the greatest gift of all. But she is bored by it. She is bored, in fact, by every finger on her hand. Bored by the drudgery of being richly blessed.

Well, so be it. She cannot sleep and trying to will make no difference. So she swings her legs out of her bed, brushes her rumpled nightshift down to her ankles and creeps, bare-footed, on the dormitory's timber floor, past the row of deep-in-slumber beds, towards the door and out into the liberties of night, where, at least, she'll not be plagued by coos and snores. She squats out of sight of any prying eyes behind the wind-break row of firs and urinates, silently and pleasingly, into the soft carpet of needles and cones, sending up the smell of resin and a warm mist. It is as if the earth is thanking her. Now that's a stream that truly never dries but pumps out an endless flow, she thinks, and is delighted with the blasphemy. She'll say as much – behind her hand – next time an angel preaches about the infinite stream of eternity. Live for ever; always need a pee. While she has been just a few moments earlier unaccountably dismayed about the life she is obliged to live unceasingly, she now is just as unaccountably cheered up. The mysteries of time and being in these celestial realms are great but none so great or unaccountable as this, a woman pissing in the night, as careless as an animal and recognizing in the rising warmth and smell another life that might be possible. Her bladder and her head have cleared at once. Again she lifts up her hand in front of her face and spreads her fingers wide in silhouette against the distant sky. Five blessings? May they all be sacrificed for something else less permanent.

Tabi does not have a plan exactly, but she knows that, come what may, she will and must break free of all those sleeping doves – the angels and her siblings – and reach a place at last where she is startled and surprised, a world that is both limitless and meaningful. Beyond eden's wall. She cleans her hands in the leaf litter of the firs, exchanging the odour of angel feathers for that of the earth, and freeing her five fingers from lordly love and everlasting life, amen.

She is about to make her way back to her bed past gardeners whose dreams are not as stirring as her own when the dormitory door swings open, carefully and almost soundlessly. She shrinks back again into the shadows. Someone else has come to splash, she supposes. She'll have to sit and wait. Or else – the very thought is thrilling – the never-resting go-between has sensed her bed is empty and has come to sniff her out. He's never caught her in the night before. In her new mood, she is determined that, if he tries to grab her by the wrist, she will fend him off. Again, she imagines flipping him like a blood-filled tick into the pond or tipping him into the privy's crusted mire.

Tabi is both relieved and disappointed, though, to recognize the dark hair and heavy shoulders of Ebon. He must have woken up and found her missing for a while too long. He often reaches for her at night, sometimes to help her quell a dream, sometimes to hush her talking in her sleep, sometimes to pull the blanket over her shoulders, sometimes only to seek some comfort for himself as if just touching her will give him back his sleep. I like to know that you are there, he's often said. It is rare for them to be apart for long. Tabi wonders if she is tethered to the man by some invisible thread and that everything she does or says will tug him in her wake. There is not a place where he'll not follow her. And there is hardly a moment when he is not at hand.

Indeed, Ebon seems to spot his orchard-woman straight away. He does not hesitate at the door, sniffing the air and cocking an ear for clues, but strides at once across the yard into the gloom of the firs. I saw that you had gone, he says, as if that is all the cause he needs to interrupt his own sleep and fetch her back. And I saw you watching me today, she says, to counter him, wanting to discomfit him. Down at the pond. Just a guess. But Ebon only rocks his head and laughs. The orchard needed you, he says. More than your angel did. Our trees. Our trees were missing you.

Ebon offers her his hand. Tabi lets him pull her to her feet. We might never touch again, she thinks, and – despite the pain in her one hand – holds on for long enough to squeeze his fingers in farewell.

5

THE WINDOW SHUTTERS and the high oak doors of the greater masters' lodgings are less than half ajar, and so the only light that penetrates from the early, luke-white moon is sliced and narrow. It's downy and it's intimate in there. This pale and sombre finish to the afternoon is usually the angels' opportunity – after a day of ministry and overseeing and, for some of them, high flights into the furthest lofts of the sky – to stretch their wings and ease their backs and lose themselves in their own company or deep in their devotions. Craw time, it's called, their chance to digest what has happened in the light as well as what they've eaten. So, despite his undoubted usefulness and the entertainment he provides unwittingly at more communal times, the feathered brethren are not pleased when, at dusk on the day when the jack is buried and when the gardeners will be summoned for their dusting down in the holier pavilions, their brief rest is interrupted by Alum calling out to them with such excessive urgency. He stands, a little out of breath – he's almost run there from the orchard and the jack's disposal in the earth – in the centre of the hay-deep floor, his body picked out by the slanting shards of moonlight and waits for their permission to report.

He is ignored, at first. Certainly, none of his masters voice any welcome. For Alum it has been so far a day without a single greeting. Let him do without. Why should the mighty angels stir at their roosts for him? Some of them muff their ears to shut out his voice. The man could at least respect their privacy, their overwhelming need to sleep, and shuffle back outdoors. But no, he calls again or, rather, coughs to draw attention to himself. No habitants ought to draw attention to themselves in the presence of their betters. How many times must they repeat that simple commandment before it is obeyed by everyone? Still the angels will not disturb their snoozes. They are relieved when, unexpectedly, Jazib, the mightiest of them all in both span and standing, takes it upon himself to hop across their perches and give voice to their impatience and anxiety. He has a bone to pick with Alum anyway, and it amuses him to tease the man and bully him. This is worth waking for.

Normally, despite the smell, Alum would enjoy the semi-darkness and his audience, his chance to air the gleanings of his day, his opportunity to be amongst the angels if not one of them. This evening, though, he is unnerved to be faced only by Jazib, the grandest inquisitor of all, and so thoroughly ignored by the others. As far as he can tell, the flock of mighty brethren have either taken wing or are huddled at the far end of the lofts, keeping as still and silent as they can while their superior takes charge. Alum can sense some of these other angels listening and fears that, somehow, he's on trial. There is the faintest scrape of talons on wood and the fluffing of feathers, the preening of a tail or the folding of a wing.

Jazib dips his head down from his perch and stretches his neck until his face is far too close for the go-between to watch both eyes at once. It's too alarming to be intimate. You've let us down. Redeem yourself. Discover quickly what occurred with Tabi, and be sure of what you find, he instructs, snapping his great wings with such power and impatience that the squall of air they cause is blustery enough to ruffle Alum's hair and lift the lappets on his cloak. Alum knows this is no time to offer his reply and to report the defiance he believes he's spotted in the orchardman's eye. He has already practised what to say: that Ebon's in the grip of disobedience, building up the courage to transgress in some dramatic way, some petulance, some sullen breaking of the rules, some foolish and destructive act. The black-haired orchardman is moping like a swan that's lost its mate. We all know why.

Discover it quickly, Jazib says again, but more softly and with greater menace, not seeking a reply but silence only, and obedience. You understand? Don't fail again.

53

We cannot tolerate . . . He lets his sentence hang unfinished in the air. He means they cannot tolerate the flouting or the loosening of rules. Their power is diminished by the missing woman. So is their meagre labour force. She has made fools of them. They also mean they cannot tolerate a go-between who does not do his job.

Alum smells the nutty taint of grain-cake on Jazib's breath, the dull, stale odour of plumage and, further off, along the perch, the chalky fust of droppings. But the greater smell is sweat. His own. He's rarely felt this scared before. Fear breaks his speech in pieces. The angel's expression is unfamiliar and threatening. This is anger, red in bill and claw, but made all the more alarming by the seeming glee in the master's eye. For a moment, Alum expects the great beak, which now is just a reach away, to come crashing down onto his head, spilling everything inside, or that the angel's talons will stretch out to slash his face and open up his chest, fulfilling every prophecy. He is as helpless as a pigeon to the angel's peregrine. He does what no servant ever should when faced with fury of this kind. He flinches and he steps away, before the angel says he can. He stumbles, almost purposely, wanting for the moment to seem clumsy, frail and deserving of pity. His heels are tangled by the hay and, impossibly, by the narrow bands of moonlight, which splinter, shorten and collapse as his body tumbles. He lands heavily on his buttocks and there is laughter from the dark ends of the lofts.

54

Alum is not granted the chance just yet to crawl away towards the door. Jazib has joined him on the lodging's floor with a floating, subtle landing – airy, almost – and has him pinned to the ground by his spreadeagled legs. The angel's not as heavy as he looks but still his grip is firm and menacing. His talons dent the soft flesh of his snitch's thighs. Find out, the master says once more, closing the gap between their two faces and tapping Alum's nose with his bill, just playfully at first – but then less playfully. The second blow is sharp enough to break the skin and raise a ruby smudge. No servant should step back like that without permission and expect to walk away without a painful reprimand. The angel's beak is tipped with blood. He wipes it on his breast. A peregrine would not stop there.

Some of the other angels have come forward from their loft, just to see what damage has been done. The smell of blood is irresistible, a far-flung memory for them but still alluring. The greatest angel lets his quarry go. Again he spreads and snaps his wing-tips like a switch, sending Alum back outside into the dusk, aided by their mocking, rageful turbulence.

IT'S MIDNIGHT NOW, and Alum – after another evening spent alone, too disturbed to deal with light and company, or even food, although the morrow is a fasting day – is safely in his bed but trembling. He knows he will not sleep, at least not for a while. His breathing is too fast and pounding. He is not only shaken by his encounter in the roosts but also – mostly – fearful of the challenges ahead. He folds his arms and brings his knees up to his chest to gain himself a little warmth and comfort in what is otherwise – or so it seems for the moment – a cold, incessant life, without pleasures or rewards and made tolerable only by the shortness of their memories. A man who isn't liked can always hug himself while he forgets. For once – it is the fleetest foolishness, quickly banished from his thoughts – he wonders if the outside world, for all its perils and its deaths, is easier than eden and eternity. Perhaps those few who've broken out into the world – from Eve to Tabi, if that indeed is where she is – are happier than he is now, despite their awful transience and ageing.

He has never felt so lonely or so fearful for himself. How tempting it would be, if he had any friends, to shake awake the neighbours in the nearest beds and whisper his concerns – and have them dress his little wound, perhaps. It's sore and sticky with blood. But, no, the heavy breathing in the dormitory, the snuffles and the snores, the creaking of the bed frames and the wheezing of the mattresses – all are a chorus of exclusion. No one there would rather sit with him than sleep.

This much is obvious: the problem of the missing woman will come between himself and heaven if he cannot act with speed. He's felt the weight of the angels'

56

displeasure on his thighs, a rare and more than intimate experience with one of the lord's most cherished adherents — What other man could make that claim? What other man would want to? — but it has not been flattering or exalting, just belittling. He should only count himself as lucky that his skin was not punctured by Jazib's talons. The beak wound on his nose should be taken as a warning. A foretaste, yes, of deeper injuries. Again, he should be grateful that he hasn't lost an eye. He shakes his head to drive away the memory. The more he thinks about the encounter in the angels' lodgings, the more he sees himself spreadeagled on the ground. The greater, priestly angels gather round, all six or seven of them, and one by one they take their turns to peck. He's like a carcass that is tugged apart by rooks. He has to shake his head again before his brain and entrails spill. Another image torments him at once. The orchardman has found Alum's corpse and buried him beneath a pile of windfalls. The go-between is trapped beneath the earth and fruit. The jack's reclining by his side, as cold and silent as a log.

Alum no longer even tries to sleep but lies awake in his chill bed to contemplate the coming day. He composes himself with measured breathing for a while until his trembling stops and he is calm enough to make decisions. His best way forward is to do exactly what Jazib demands: find this Tabi or, at the least, find out where and how she got away. Discover quickly; and be sure of it? That's not as easy as it sounds.

So he is up and out at dawn, despite his weariness, tracing what he hopes were Tabi's recent steps. He is the first to leave the dormitory, and he is more careful than usual not to wake his fellows. In normal times, he'd bang the footboards of their beds or pinch their toes just to make them spill their dreams. But it's best if he's not noticed. He has been pecked and shamed. The bridge of his nose is red and sore, a wound it's better no one notices and asks about. The truth will only make him seem less deserving of respect.

As usual, he pushes his squeaky barrow and carries his trug, disguising his true purposes from anyone who might pass by later in the day. What are his purposes? He'll be methodical, that's all he knows. The search must begin within the garden wall. Climbing and then crossing that rampart, let alone just touching it, would be such a blasphemy that it is almost inconceivable that anyone might try. Even Tabi. The scriptures record that the lord built that wall himself, stone upon stone: who else would have the strength to lift such mighty blocks? So it's as sacred as it is forbidden. Therefore, it's still a possibility that Tabi has not taken flight beyond the holy battlement entirely but is simply hiding within their bounds, concealing some resentment from the angels or her fellows. It's not unknown for a brother or a sister to slip away to brew a grievance for a day or two, hidden in a cupboard or a cellar or a lumber shed, and then show up again, shame-faced, disarmed and hungry, ready to apologize and eat. Some imagined grudge might have sent Tabi off to sulk in private. Not many days have passed since Alum himself was obliged to twist back her juicy fingers and rescue those tomatoes for the common table. She's always been the thin-skinned sort of soul who'd not forgive that readily, he thinks. Tabi might not have gone beyond the wall at all but stayed within the garden, leading her eternal life but out of sight.

His starting point must be the orchard where she works. He stands a good way off at the gateway to the fruit fields and carefully checks each treetop for some movement or shape that's bigger than a squirrel or a bird, or for some flash of orange from her shawl. But even though the sun is high enough to light and aid his search, there is no sign of her amongst her trees. It's early still. The orchardman's not out and working yet. But the birds have left their roosts already and seem undisturbed. They would not seem so casual if there were a climber in the branches. Jack-chat, jack-chat, they'd say. Beware. Nor are there footprints through the grass, as there might be if she had spent the night-time hiding there. None of the morning dew has been shaken from the stem except where Alum himself has walked and where he's squeaked his barrow.

It's possible that Tabi might have fallen from a treetop perch, he thinks – and almost hopes. That certainly would simplify his task. No one could blame him for a fall. After all, she lives a reckless, carefree life and could be lying on the earth, bruised and broken, her ankles snapped perhaps, not conscious possibly but warm and breathing like a winter hedgehog, waiting to be found as soon as it is day. The orchard and the nuttery are so wide and dense, a body could be missed. Even her fawner Ebon might not have discovered her yet. All that Alum has to do is to be the one to sniff her out and bring her home triumphantly, folded in his barrow like a sack of moist straw. He can imagine, standing in the hay below the lofts, displaying her, his dignity regained. Will he dare to point at her and ask, Whose fault is this? Not mine! Not mine! But, once again, though he circles round and checks beneath most of the trees and even delves into the deepest clenches of the undergrowth, there is no sign of her.

Alum's surprised how thwarted and dejected he now feels at this first disappointment. He worries sometimes that he, just like everybody else, or so it seems, is in the woman's thrall, more fascinated than repelled by her, and by the challenge that she offers him. If she were as biddable as all the other women in the garden, he'd not pay her any heed. But he can't ignore her waywardness. It has crossed his mind many times to ask the angels if they would assign Tabi to his side, as his trug-bearer and subordinate, all the better to control each moment of her day. His heart beats faster just at the thought of it, of having her company from dawn to dusk, of watching her from just a step or two behind as she struggles with his barrow and its squeaking wheel. He could pull her bed up close to his own at the far end of the dormitory and listen to her every breath at night. And listen to her every word by day. She is diverting, certainly, though much of what she says is wild. Her every sentence is a tease. Yet, if she were assigned to him and was known not as the orchardman's but as the go-between's, she might be tamed. The truth is, Alum wants her for himself, if only as a trophy. If he has been cruel to her, almost cracking the bones in her fingers, it's not because of his regard for rules – or even for tomatoes – but because it is a thrill for such a lonely man to hold her fiercely in his hands.

He spends the next part of the morning, though now less high with hope and hastened by foreboding, sniffing out her hiding places away from the orchard. He hurries towards the cluster of buildings, but, when he passes within sight of the stock pond, he, on a hunch, walks down to the water's edge. That feeble angel, Jamin, who has himself attempted foolishly to cross the garden's boundaries and is still malingering with what he claims is damage to his wing, has a shady bower there where he consorts with all the garden's invalids and weaklings, a monarch amongst his minnows, both in the water and out of it. Tabi was with him there the day before she disappeared, paying more attention to his plumage than she should. He spotted them himself and noted their too comfortable collusion. Alum will not be surprised to find her nestled in the bower under a blanket of moulted feathers. But there is nobody around, not even Jamin himself, who at this time before the sun is giving out much heat will still be fussing in his loft. There are, though, insects on the pond, and something in the marshy margins that could be a vole or rat but only for the blink of an eye could be mistaken for a woman. An egret, whiter than a snowdrop, is frightened off by the barrow's squeak before it has a chance to fish. But otherwise the only beating heart is Alum's own.

Now, already dispirited, he visits the furthest granges, snouts in the deepest underbrush, pokes his long-handled trowel into the darkest crevices. He lifts the wooden covers on the garden wells and, after first making sure that no one is in earshot, echoes Tabi's name into the dripping darkness. He checks the hay and silage lofts and all the timber stores and peers into the under-crofts and cellars, not stepping in because the water there is ankle deep and not a place where anyone might hide, unless they were a lizard or a frog. He probes the undergrowth and overyawns around the huddled nave of buildings at the garden's hub, disturbing only birds and bats. Then he ventures down the slypes which lead between pavilions into the cloister yards, where he prays – and is rewarded for it – that there will be no angels to question him or wonder at his prying.

He is, in many ways, a trespasser. Being there, at this

time of the day, is not forbidden, but it is discouraged. These holy spaces are not meant for him. But, still, he circles all the pillars and the posts, watching out for shadows and listening for scurries, and pushes back the squeaking cedar doors into the robing room in case his woman is denning there, a fleshy moth amongst the cloaks and vestments. He even breaks unspoken rules and opens all the aumbries in the prayer rooms and the cupboards in the chapel, where absurdly – inexplicably – the holy relics, censers and ancient rosaries are left to mould and rust. He peers into any space that is big and dry enough to make a den; the stock house and the chapter house, the angels' parlour and the campanile.

He is surprised by what he finds: a hoard of nuts and seeds that some thief has squirrelled in a box, a stash of pots, sticky with honey, a sack of tiny bones, a shiny knife, more ornamented than his own and which he is tempted to take for himself, a chest packed tight with embroidered bedding, never used, some silver chalices, a pair of iron anklets with a length of leather strapping and some heavy chain, a wasps' nest in a gable end, all sorts of trinkets in an earth, dragged in by foxes possibly or rats. It certainly is stinking there. He has to brush the droppings from his hands and knees. And sticky spider webs, together with the dusty frass of lattice flies, the detritus of lice.

Finally, cushioned in a little moleskin purse at the bottom of a scripture chest, he retrieves somebody's hidden or forgotten treasure trove of polished stones. He licks a couple of them clean and turns them on his palm. They catch whatever light there is, rewarding him with colours he could never find in the garden, even in the flowerbeds. He hesitates but only for a moment. These gems might make quite useful gifts. Or bribes. If he is to lose the benefit of angels, as does not seem unlikely, it might be wise to cultivate some wingless friends at last, a few confederates who will judge it worth their whiles to let him join their conversations or welcome him to eat his suppers at their sides. He knows he ought to use his smile a little more and call upon his fists much less. These bright stones can be his solid smiles. Who wouldn't want one in their pocket, for good luck? Or underneath their pillow, glinting light into their dreams? He checks again that he is not being watched, then ties the purse onto the lanyard underneath his armpit on the inside of his cloak. He has not stolen them, he's rescued them, he's made them purposeful. His spirits have been lifted by his find. But signs of Tabi? There are none.

One final search: the living rooms. Everyone is up and out by now and so he has the buildings to himself. He pushes back the door into the privies and even — quickly — looks down into the drop. He spits and sends up clouds of flies. He checks the cupboards and the roof-beam storage spaces where the bedding spares are kept. In the dormitory, he throws back any mattresses that look too deep or bulky and could conceal a body, asleep or otherwise. He calls her name in all directions, just to fill the room with it. Finally, down on his hands and knees, he peers beneath Tabi's bed, praying for but no longer truly expecting any evidence of her disloyalty, such as the remains of a severed rope or signs of stored supplies. She might have scratched her mark into the headboard of the bed, a farewell note or a scar of discontent, he thinks. But no. There's not the faintest spraint of her.

Alum does not lift his head to face his disappointment but presses his wounded nose into Tabi's bed, wanting nothing more than sleep, that short-lived unconsciousness, his only respite from eternity. He had so little in the night. He is surprised to trace the faintest smell of her, her body, on the coverlets and pillow, no stronger than a mallow's, a flimsy stirring of the senses, just a provocation and a hint. But smelling her just once like this removes the trace of her entirely from the bed. He cannot find her there again. She's in his nostrils now, his memory. He has her like a hound has quarry before the hunt begins.

At last Alum stands and stretches his limbs now to accept the greater, shocking likelihood and act on it. As everybody who has known her and has laboured with her has suspected from the moment she went missing from her bed, Tabi will not be discovered within their wall, hiding in some sullen hole or tucked like pillows in a chest, any more than she could have been found deep in bushes underneath an orchard tree, with a broken leg or back, as he has so recently thought possible. She's committed a great profanity and has slipped outside into the world, somehow, and has done so without warning. And, for that, Alum will have to accept the burden of blame. That much is clear. He really can't complain. The masters have a right to wonder why, of all the people on the lord's estate, Tabi has not been under constant watch. As Alum has reported many times himself, she is the garden's loudest mouth. He has recounted to them, word for word, her mocking of their articles of faith, that they are all a pack of lies. And he has often been reminded in their replies that the lord is as displeased with her as he is affronted by those garden tares and docks that will not propagate as he desires but rather are uncultured and unruly. They should be weeded out.

But Alum has been slow to weed her out. There's no denying it. He knows the trouble that she spreads like muck around the roots and boots of all the garden-hands, but he has been reluctant to silence her. The most he's done is to brush her lips and stop her wrist when she was stealing from his trug. Otherwise, he's been too indulgent. She's been allowed to live her life unhindered mostly. Uninterrupted also. Even when she's mouthing nonsense to her siblings – her incitements and her fantasies seem to know no bounds – when she should be staying quiet, he has only listened with a careful grimace of disapproval on his face but not silenced her or reported what she's said to the masters. He's keen to give them the impression that he has the measure of the woman when, sadly, he has not. But still he plays her lightly with the angels – for she is his, not theirs.

So, yes, Alum has been negligent and now must bear the weight of it. He puts his hand up to his face and feels the swelling and the forming scab where he's been pecked. He shudders at the prospect of another wound. The masters always like to leave a mark. Perhaps, if he disappoints them yet again, they'll want to choose another man to be their go-between, their honoured snitch. His job is just a brevet after all, as easy to take away now as it was to award in his ascendancy. A new name will be spoken of and respected in the heavens. And Alum's restful occupation of hardly doing anything all day apart from collecting vegetables and keeping his eyes open might be gifted to another. The angels' nose, their eyes, their ears, is not expected – not allowed, indeed – to be as deaf and blind as everybody else. He should have heard and seen what Tabi had in mind. He means to catch her, come what may. He will hold her fiercely in his hands again.

6

IT IS A fasting but still a working day for Ebon and like no other he has known. He is alone in his labours and has been so for, what? Four days? He isn't used to counting time, any more than he is used to weighing the air he breathes. He has to tally on his fingers how many nights he's spent with a cold and silent bed next to his own and how many times, waking in the muffled darkness, he has had to reach across to check its covers are no longer shaped by Tabi. The silent hollow of her mattress is equalled by the beating hollow of his heart. It feels as if he has to breathe for both of them. Once or twice, unable to gain the haven of sleep, he hears the sister on the other side of Tabi's bed reaching out as well. He feels the draught of her deep breaths on his damp cheeks and then more draughts as the covers are swished aside by an out-stretched hand and explored for any warmth, and finally her sigh. She's sighing not only for a missing friend but for the years that lie ahead and no longer feel secure.

All Ebon knows is that time is standing still, that those busy, cheerful, quickly passing moments that comprised his working life when she was at his side have grown long and tedious. His angel says that if there is another hand to spare, once the grain crops have been harvested elsewhere in the lord's fields, he will replace – replant is the actual word he uses – the missing woman, the fugitive, the runagate. But replanting her is not the same as having her. A tree that's bountiful with seasons and fully fledged and rooted, as Tabi was, is not matched by some sapling. That would be only a frail reminder of what greater planting has once flourished there.

So Ebon has to brace himself against the prospect of working side by side with someone whom he doesn't love as much and has not learnt to trust. At least, if the angel keeps his word, as angels are expected to, he'll then have help at the fast-approaching bedding time, when all the orchard is picked clean and raked bare, made cosy for the winter, left virgin for the coming spring. But for the moment he must labour without company.

It's dull. But he can manage everything alone and always could. Tabi has never been the best of workers, though she could be the noisiest. Ebon has teased her for it countless times. She does not concentrate for long, even with her very favourite tasks. What she likes most is clambering amongst the branches to chop out dead or excess wood or to pluck and save the highest, plumpest fruit from falling and bruising. Often, needing help with the raking or the mulching on the ground, he has called her name a dozen times before she shouted his in reply from the high crown of a tree, entirely hidden by the leaves. She's still pollarding, she says, or pairing heads of fruit for that year's harvest, or pruning spurs, or notching bark up there. There's always some excuse for staying in the crown, for remaining mistress of the tops for yet another afternoon.

She's careless too, and inconsiderate. Indeed, once in a while, an offcut of her high labour — some twigs, some unformed pears, edible as pebbles, and sometimes, madly, even a heavy limb that she has dehorned and let go — comes crashing to the ground too close to Ebon's feet. He might curse, but she will only laugh, delighted by the drama of their day. More often, when her silence rather than her clamour worries him, he steps into open ground to get a clearer view, until he catches sight of her protruding head staring at the far too distant world but perched on branches that seem barely strong enough to bear the weight of fruit, let alone a gardener. She's more a squirrel than a tabitha, he thinks, although she is as restless as a deer once she's descended from a tree. If she had longer ears, they would be wary, twitching and alert all day, intrigued by everything they heard. She has always been what Ebon calls a bouncing breeze, that is a person whose vivacity can make the leaves rustle and cause the trees themselves to creak and sough at her coming and departing.

In this, too often, Tabi is exasperating. One person's bouncy breeze can be another's squall. She is ill-tempered far too frequently, and then her tongue is sharper than the snitch's knife. Stay clear of her barbed and pointed blade. She chatters to herself, like an agitated bird. She has her moods, some sunny and others chilly as the moon, though there's no telling when they might rise or set. She helps herself to anything that's edible, both at the table and away from it. She snores. She steals. She laughs too readily, sometimes without good cause or any cause that's she's prepared to share. She seems to think it is her duty to oppose the masters and their ministry but not her duty to be dutiful. She is too often bored by her protected life and so she longs to see the outside world and, she says, might rather stare death in the eye, whatever it might prove to be, than live forever and as blindly as she must within their boundaries. She's frightening, in that. Ebon has had to ask her to hush a thousand times.

She's not alone in wanting her horizons to expand beyond the wall despite what they are told in sermons: Limits make community, and It is the wall that keeps you free: the greater its height, the more protected are your liberties. But free from what? they wonder. From heartless magnitude, they're told. From vastness and immensity. From space that is as everlasting out there as time is never-ending in the lord's estate. And then the angels warn – and boast – about the stretching, pitiless, outside world that they have witnessed from above, on wing,

71

how there are deserts and great glaring blocks of ice, ten times the size of eden, how there are mountains higher than the clouds, how oceans – compared to which Jamin's stock pond is a tear-drop or a bead of sweat – lap against the shore, removing it, returning it, with never-idling waves. It is a world where beasts are running free and wild, with bloodied fangs, where there is pain and pestilence, where – instead of being fashioned by the lord, everlasting and immaculate – the people that are bound to die are also bound to reproduce themselves amongst themselves, like animals. Their little saplings writhe and feed as helplessly as tadpoles in a pond, then crawl like worms, then tremble on their legs once they begin to stand, then run around as madly as geese, before they learn to disobey and fight, and even then they are no use to their mothers or their fathers in the workshops or the fields. No, fifty seasons have to pass before they're wise enough or tall enough to be of any use. These are a people who commence their span soft and weak and finish it gnarled and weak. Brief life is all they have out there, the sermonizing master says. Brief sorrow and brief care. And suffer them to shiver and to starve. Misfortune has made those creatures on the far side of the wall to be forever lesser than the habitants of eden as moths are lesser than birds. And birds are lesser than angels, come to that. And you are happy, are you not, the master asks, to have such providence? Yes, they nod, we must be so.

72

No matter who the angel is, he lifts and stretches both his wings at this point in the sermon to mime the width of their good fortune and to remind his congregation of their contented lives, the permanence they enjoy. If you leave here, you will be lost, he says. They chorus their agreement and their thanks, though many wonder what it must be like to leave, to go away and then be lost amongst the children and the deserts and the beasts. It is only Tabi who has the nerve — or is it foolishness — to mutter, just a little too out loud, that the angels are deceiving them. Just fairy-tales to frighten fools like us. Great blocks of ice, ten times the size of eden? What might be the point of that? Vast shoreless ponds? Mountains that are tall enough to stare down on the clouds? Well, seeing is believing, as far as I'm concerned, she says. Just let me plant my foot on them. Her fellows turn their backs on her. She is the only fool, they think, to doubt an angel's word.

Still, there's not a man or woman within the lord's estate who wouldn't want to work with Tabi at their side, if she were not already Ebon's constant daytime partner, for being close to her and her itchy feet is as close as anyone might get to being far from eden. And there isn't one of them who does not try to sit beside her at the table after work, hoping that their arms and hers, their knees and hers, might touch as they throw back their heads to laugh out loud at something she has said or done. Those soft collisions of the limbs are satisfying for them all but unaccountably embarrassing. They're immodest and forbidden. Knees and ankles are hurriedly drawn back and faces lowered by way of an apology.

Tabi's not embarrassed, though. Nor timid. Nor obedient. She loves to snub her nose against the etiquettes. When rules are recited after prayer – No one should talk or laugh during services, for example, or All should cast down their eyes when meeting with a master, or None should hasten in an undignified manner when the summons bell is heard – many of those congregated there, including some angels, will smile and try to catch their Tabi by the eye, complicitly. They know she'll not be stifled by a rule.

So at the table, each and every evening other than on fast days, Tabi eats as if no order governs her, except the law of common sense and appetite that requires each scrap of food to be well chewed, including some, it must be said, that might be idling or neglected on a neighbour's plate. Beware her fingers and her knife. Just watch the way she holds her cup, despite the custom that demands she should use only her fingertips. Just see her sitting, chin in hand, or arms spread out across the table when a greater neatness of composure is required. Just watch her eating without temperance and far too cheerfully, when everybody else is modest, quiet and sparing, shielding their enjoyment with a hand. Daily eating is a duty, not a feast, the angels say. Greed is lacking in

74

respect. Be humble, frugal and restrained before your food. Rise from the table just a little underfed.

Tabi, naturally, is not restrained or underfed in anything she does or says. Sometimes it's hard, even for Ebon, not to find her mischievous and tiresome, but she is easy to forgive and harder to forget. She is a story in herself, someone has said, a tale to tell admiringly in whispers when she's not there to scoff at it or contradict. None will forget – because it is so frequently retold – that joyful, discomfiting occasion at winter's end when against all normal practices – against all higher principles, indeed – an angel came into the refectory on a working day while everyone was eating. Rather than withdrawing as he should have done, he called across the table to Tabi and requested that she visit him whenever she was free, to aid him with his yearly moult. His plumage was eclipsing – always a shame-faced time for angels – and she might like to help him to loosen and remove those feathers that were moribund and good only for a pillow or a hat. The diners all cast down their eyes, excepting Tabi. She shuffled her bottom along the supper bench and invited the angel – it was Jamin, in times before the damaged wing – to join the gathering. And he did so! A shocking lapse. Their jaws hung open, heavy with surprise and half-chewed food. He perched, as best he could, amongst them at the table and Tabi – winking at anyone who dared look up – gained a little extra warmth for herself by sitting close, her shoulder pressed against his wing, a curl of mischief on her lips. She even, to a chorus of gasps, held up her plate for him to peck at anything he liked, as if he were no grander than a pigeon or a cat. It wasn't long before a second person, then a dozen more, found the nerve to slide some scraps across to him, some honeyed cake, some crusts of bread and even wedges of potato, cooked in cumin, mint and dill – or Justice, Mercy and Faithfulness, as they are called in scriptures, where every herb and spice has attributes. It was an ecstatic evening, though brief. Imagine it: an angel at the table, flank to hip with everyone, heaven's feathers touching their unholy skin. Despite the unease everybody felt at first, there was soon laughter in the room, such happiness and such hilarity.

Alum was the only one to stand and leave the feast, a smear of gravy and a rictus of disapproval unwiped from his face. The refectory was silenced by the thunder of his parting and then again by the inevitable lightning of Jamin's immediate alarm. The angel, fearing for himself and for Tabi, jumped at once with hardly a moment's hesitation onto the tabletop, leaving moulted feathers on the bench where he had perched at Tabi's side. Knocking plates and dishes sideways as he fled, tipping bottles, spilling sauce and sending walnuts rolling on the floor, he scampered after Alum to the door.

Everybody half expected – and half hoped – there to be a rare commotion in the darkness outside, if the lord's least respected angel caught up with his most respected

76

snitch before he could inform the priests in their lofts that rules that night were broken. It was impossible even to guess what sort of confrontation there might be and which of them would prevail. It was exciting, though, to imagine a duel of fist and claw, of squawking and of cussing. For once, the diners favoured angel over man, the moulting wing against the greater arm. They held their breaths and strained their ears. Even Tabi managed to stay quiet. Ebon had placed his hand on her arm and drummed advice with his fingertips. She understood it wasn't wise to laugh, even though her instincts said she should. But, no, there was no commotion outside their feasting room other than the wind, the bats, the creaking timbers and the banging far away of an unfastened gate. Whoever left that gate unlatched did not dare to run and fix it yet.

No one truly knows if Jamin and Alum ever came to blows or if they even spoke that night. There were rumours and tall tales – but no evidence. Bubbles but no fish, as Jamin himself might say. Probably, they simply went their ways, alone. Certainly, next day, the pair who helped Jamin at the stock pond did not find him crestfallen. He'd not been punished or reproved. An angel is beyond the law. But nobody doubted what Tabi's punishment might be once word of her unruly feast reached disapproving ears in those dark lofts, how she had trifled with Jamin, how she had fed him like a cat, how he'd trifled with Justice, Mercy and Faithfulness, encouraged by her devilry, how he had clambered onto the tabletop with help from her to desecrate the altar of the meal. For this, she wasn't easy to forgive. They summoned her, they preached at her, they punished her. She was excluded until the next rest day from all meals and meetings, and she was silenced for the week. Scraps were gifted to her by her friends or left beneath her bedclothes each of the seven nights so that she wouldn't have to sleep and dream with hunger as her mate.

Jamin has never dined with them again. But his one visit to the refectory is still talked about, though time has made all of its participants more carefree and heroic than they really were. According to the story that they tell themselves, they all sat close to him and felt his warmth; they all held up their plates and shared their suppers with the angel; there was not a single one of them who was fearful, not one of them who cried Innocent or tried to shift the blame when Alum came the next day to challenge them and tell them that the angels were displeased. In their retelling, everyone was spirited and brave.

NOW EBON, STANDING alone in the orchard just a step or so away from the freshly dug ground with its ghostly cloud of predatory gnats where only yesterday the jack was buried, cannot help but smile when he remembers all the mayhem Tabi caused on that happy, troubled evening. He stretches out his hand and drums his fingers on the smooth bark of a newly grafted tree, as if he's hushing it, as he has had to hush her many times. He takes his pruning knife and carves an oval in the bark, above a smudge of orange lichen which can stand as Tabi's shawl. Then he stabs and gouges in her eyes and ears and nose and mouth and slashes lines to represent her hair. This portrait in their orchard of his orchard-sister might be rough and hurried, lacking in expression, but it will last for so many seasons more than the like-nesses that people carve into the skins of pumpkins or of marrows and that, though they are quick to swell and gurn, rarely survive the harvest or a frost. Bark faces never leave their trees, although it could take a dozen years before her face expands, her smile broadens and her eyes are entirely open. Then he can watch her watching him.

So it is for Tabi – a tribute, actually – wherever she might be, apart from etched into the bark, that Ebon, a dutiful and timid man in normal times, decides to be as bold as her for once and to snub his nose against a rule. He stoops and picks up from the burial ground one of the windfalls clustered there. Purposely, he ignores the pears and summer's final plums and chooses an apple that is bruised and split and has already been pecked out by birds. There are gashes in the skin. Fids of flesh mark where beaks have struck. It isn't truly edible. He holds it up to Tabi on the bark to show her he is not timid any more. The angels' teachings on the matter are quite clear. No fallen fruit in eden – excepting nuts, which must not be tugged from their stems but allowed to drop like blessings in the lord's good time – should ever be consumed by sister or by brother, and certainly not on a fasting day such as this when any eating is prohibited. They have fallen from grace and now are nothing more than the sweepings of the orchard-floor, the strew and debris of the trees. They have been compromised by sawfly, scab and coddling moths and blemished by the earth, and so are counted as unclean, as rotten to the core as any sinner ever is. Indeed, they're known as sinners, scamps and scoundrels, condemned for having broken free. No, such blistered fruit is good only for burying or composting. Or for animals and alms.

They've been good enough for Tabi, though. Ebon's seen her countless times stoop down just as he is doing now to save an apple from the jacks, or to retrieve plums or pears or apricots, or perry crabs, or bullaces, depending on the season. Even in the winter he has caught her wincing on a fallen gage that somehow has survived the cold. She mostly takes only one deep, defiant bite before throwing the remains as far as they will go. Sometimes she bares her teeth and opens up the flesh, just for the fun of it. So sweet, she says, spitting out the pips or picking bits from between her teeth. Or, That one's reasty, that one's hardly ripe, that one's far too good for birds. More than once she hasn't noticed there's a wasp, too drunk on fruit to get away, and has cried out with pain at its reproving sting inside her mouth. Were any angels watching, or their go-between? Tabi never checks or cares. So what if I'm excluded yet again from meals and prayers? she says, talking wildly. There are always scamps and scoundrels to eat, out in the gardens, meadows and orchards. And prayers? Well, prayers are not as sweet as apples, anyway. A prayer cannot be half eaten, then sent spinning through the air. A prayer does not have pips to spit. You couldn't heel a prayer into the ground and hope for it to turn into a tree.

It is, though, with foreboding that Ebon lifts his windfall – a scarred and mottled cooker, already russeted with mould – to his mouth. He rests his teeth upon it, hesitates. He hardly recognizes himself. He has always been respectful of the rules. It is his nature to collaborate, not contravene. This trembling man whose teeth are poised to do the devil's work can hardly be the Ebon of old. He has a sudden image of himself lying prostrate in front of his fellows and the angels, begging their forbearance. He has tasted the forbidden fruit and knows he'll have to pay the price. He throws his head back, aghast at what he is about to do, but frightened that he'll lose his nerve. And, hardly knowing it or meaning it, as if his jaw is something other than his own, he splits the apple's outer skin. At once he tastes the sour, over-sweetened bruising in the flesh. There's no resistance to his teeth. The innards are as soft as curd, as pungent brown as carrion. Even Tabi would not have persevered with it. Ebon, though, has made a compact with her memory. He plunges further in until his mouth is puffed with apple meat, the bitter, corky pith and scent of death. He senses too what Tabi's always known: the fizzing sugars of a rotting fruit are, like some forest 'rooms and 'stools, powerful and heady. He has often found her, after three or four of the mushiest, laughing inexplicably, and at other times made drowsy, and at others quarrelsome. Even with that single bite, Ebon tastes a trace and promise of something that could make him difficult and troublesome. Now he feels, at once, both lost and found, both tainted and redeemed. No wonder that the masters rule the windfalls aren't for eating. Ebon swallows most of his mouthful. He spits the rest, a globby mass that does not travel far.

Ebon sweeps his tongue into the corners of his mouth until all taste and trace of apple are removed. Only now he looks around and listens hard, half expecting to see moving shadows in the nuttery and to hear the squeaking of a barrow's wheel. But all is well. Another windfall crashes at his feet. Another sinner falls from grace. A shriven bough adjusts itself with every impulse of the wind. The branches bicker and complain. The orchard's busy still with jacks. It is elating that he does not feel regretful yet or anything other than well.

He does feel guilty, though. He could be walking back to his bed by now and washing off the dirt of day before a fasting afternoon of rest, but he wants to hide himself a little longer. He's never truly sinned before and fears that sin will wear itself across his cheeks, the hot, fermenting blush of shame, for everyone to see and comment on. The trees forgive him. They don't judge. They cannot smell or taste. They're deaf and blind and have no memory. He looks upon them as fondly as he looks upon his siblings. They fascinate and baffle him. For all his care, his expertise and his diligence, the orchard is unknowable. Tabi has often laughed at Ebon for caring for his trees so much. You love them more than anything, she says. And anyone? He shakes his head. And anyone? she asks again.

7

FASTING DAYS ARE normally looked forward to, despite the empty stomachs and the thirst. The habitants are allowed to finish work much earlier than usual. There is a bell, mid-afternoon to chime them home. The lord has a bell for everything, from quarters to alarms, and somebody to ring it. Though he is distant, he sounds near. He can be deafening. This bell says they are to tidy up, clean and stow their tools, latch their gates and return to their beds for rest. There they should refresh themselves and so be eager for the morrow, which will be an ordinary day of reaching, fetching, stooping, worship, meals. But truly none of them are tired – or tired enough to waste this free time sleeping. It is a treat to be awake and idle while the sun still shines.

For most of them, despite the pestering bell, the walk from work is even slower than that morning's trudge towards it. They have the time to stop and chat, to stare each other in the face in daylight rather than in moon or candle glow or in the dismaying shadows of a lanthorn. Those who work out in the grander fields amongst the awns of wheat and rye with their far-yonder skies are at liberty to linger for a while in the snugger and more formal garden courts which the angels have called chapels – for cultivating the ground is a form of prayer, they say, if only a lowly one – and where they are free to tarry with the bees and hover flies amid the herbs and salad leaves. And, on the way, they might pass and greet the herb and lettuce gardeners who, wearied by the confines of their chapels and stiffened by so many days spent hunting weeds and slugs, are heading for the open land – the bread granges, as they're called – to see how much the grain has ripened since the previous day of fasting and to breathe unblunted air.

There will be loiterers as well down at the stock pond, where they can spend some moments spitting chewed grass for the fish, taking care not to break their fasts with so much as a mashed shred of it. They should not swallow even their own spit, they're told, so what choice is there but to hawk it out? They throw in stones, just to see the water rings expand and flatten. Jamin, the pond-keeper, doesn't seem to mind. He only watches quietly from his perch, happy in his bill and coo, his daydreaming. Of all the angels, he's the one who seems – a baffling mix – the most absorbed, the least engaged. It is as if his eyesight and his hearing are as gammy as his wing, so nothing they may do or say in front of him is either noticed or considered. They say that he can be as blind and deaf to sin as any tree.

Now the fasting bell is calling them more urgently. Their supervising angel is impatient at the dormitory door. He would like to roost himself, rather than attend the advent of these stragglers. It's not only their own time they are wasting. And so the last few workers scurry down the straight and tended walkways, between the avenue of limes which darkens to a row of unbrashed firs, planted to shield the buildings from the wind. Then they are free to face an afternoon and evening of rest without a meal. This is the time each week when everyone must wash themselves and in a holy order: toe to tip and hole to pole, as the vulgar saying goes. By the fire-log piles, there is a row of wooden laver tubs shaded by canopies. They have been bucketed with well water during the day and allowed to warm and settle. At the first tub, the fasting workers queue to brush their teeth with green hazel shoots and a cinder paste. An angel watches them; they should not swallow anything but – again – just spit it out. They stand in the second tub to clean their legs and feet and pick off any lice or fleas. The third is for their bodies, for scrubbing off the mud and sweat with wood-ash soap until their skin grins through again. Both men and women push aside their working clothes to clean their pizzles and their folds. The final basin is lined with cloth and, after each ablution, is refilled with fresh water and scented oils. This is for the hair and face and this is where their spirits are renewed and fed. There the briefly famished are baptized.

The common practices require that the newly washed should neither linger nor stray once they are dry but hurry to their sleeping places to doze or rest or, at the most, talk quietly with a neighbour. They are allowed to pray. Or pay tribute to the lord with gentle handiwork. No hammering. This is when the neighbours plait their mats and twist their ropes or stitch their clothes or weave their hats. This is the time when, over many fasting days, Alum expressed his loneliness and sorrow in the making of his trug and his barrow. Sometimes, if there is fruit to prepare or peas and beans to shell for tomorrow's meals, a couple of the less observant workers can be found sitting at the benches by the kitchen door, peeling and pulsing their devotions into a pan. They might look as pious as the seraphim, telling their prayers with pods and skins instead of strings of beads, yet they are only waiting for the chance to cheat the fast by popping something that they've shucked or cut into their pockets. Or their mouths.

These fast-day afternoons are also an opportunity – an excuse – for touching. That's a lapse, in principle. Not only dress and speech but gestures also should be modest and restrained. No one, though, can be expected to shave their own heads or tie back their own hair or weave a tidy beard when there are so many idle hands around eager to help out. If angels can be groomed and stroked and fingertipped by human hands, why cannot the gardeners be intimate amongst themselves, especially when they are washed, sweet smelling and unsoiled? So they primp and spruce each other in all innocence. They can be forgiven if they whisper as they work and share their stories, rumours and surmises, their conjectures and their false alarms, or if they give voice to grievances and gripes. Finally, tired out by idleness and liberty, most of them take refuge in their beds.

There is, though, an expedition away from the barns, lofts and pavilions anyone can take part in when work is done on fasting afternoons. It is allowed. It is encouraged even. Those who do not want to rest can devote the afternoon to charity and carry gifts and alms down to the barbican's great gates, where the gardens of the lord's estate almost touch the world, where comfort, peace and plenty very nearly brush the skin of time. They rummage in the stores and cupboards for waste food or any piece of clothing that is too worn to use or no longer fitting, or else they beg some dry bread or biscuit from the kitchen larders, or donate one of the spoons or candles or woven baskets that they've made themselves and do not truly need. They walk to the gatehouse in a slow and proud procession, comparing their gifts and their sacrifices with their neighbours' as they go. It's tempting to be thankful there are poor folk on the far side of the sacred wall. Without hunger, there can be no charity – and no expedition either. It can be a jolly time. Walking dulls their hunger. Chatting helps them to forget how thirsty they've become. Besides, it seems a waste to hide themselves away in the gloomy dormitory when they are so soaped and scrubbed and shriven of all their shortcomings.

This afternoon, they must as usual pass the fringes of the orchard as they walk and they are not surprised to notice Ebon there, hunting underneath his trees for alms. Each fasting day in season, it is his final job to gather up the least damaged of the windfalls, the tainted and forbidden fruit, and give them to the hungry souls beyond the wall. Out there, it seems, uncleanliness is nothing to be feared. An empty stomach doesn't care if apples have been pecked and bruised or riddled out by worms.

Ebon has a wooden rake to gather up the fruit. He clears the rotting apples from the jack's burial mound and slops them into his largest straw basket. Then he crouches in the under-arches of the trees and shifts around like a land crab to retrieve whatever better windfalls he can find. He is still surprised, despite the ages he has spent as the honoured and trusted orchardman, how careless apple trees can be, always shedding, always letting go. The flowers first, left pinkly brown and slushy on the ground. The spring apples next, hard as stones, but crowded off the stem by bigger ones. Then those young fruits thinned out by the gales. And after that the many summer drops, too firm and sour even for the jacks and jays. Next come the windfalls, fruit that's tasty but impatient, it would seem. Then there are those few that can't be reached at apple time, even by the squirrel woman, the lofty ones. The autumn wind will bring them down, along with every single leaf, along with laden branches even. A bough breaks loose and crashes to the ground, groaning with the heft of too much peel and pith and pip, as if its own abundance is too much to bear. Ebon wonders at the wisdom of it all. Such wantonness and waste. The angels say the lord has perfected every living thing. So why such overload?

It isn't long before the basket is misshapen by its weight of alms. The load looks generous, but Ebon is not fooled by that. And nor is Tabi, it would seem. Her bark face is unsmiling still and stern. These gifts are not attractive to the nose or eye. They stink of sweet decay and – as he knows too well; he sinned upon a windfall just a while ago – their taste is mean. He wouldn't give such damaged apples to an animal, so why should he basket them for men and women, one of whom – he cannot shake away this hope – might be Tabi? What charity is this?

So Ebon quickly breaks another rule. The second sin is always easier. The earth did not open up and swallow him with the first, when he transgressed and feasted on the cooker. And it does not open its unforgiving jaws and swallow him when he reaches up into the branches and carefully selects the very best of unpicked apples, the ones that on a normal day would be polished and presented on a tray to the highest angels or saved for feast-day baking. No matter how you turned them, they would flicker and glisten in the candlelight, like sacred altar orbs. Their skins would be so perfect and so oiled they'd reflect the angel who was eyeing them.

He frees a good score of the best from their nests of leaves – noting yet again that satisfying snap of twig from stalk, so unresisting that it's a mystery how it ever supported such a weight – and positions them across the surface of his basket until none of the bad fruit is on display. He adds a second score, just to be certain that his meanness is no longer visible. Who does he think he's fooling, other than himself?

The basket is unusually heavy, and Ebon, as he hauls it up onto his shoulders and begins the walk down to the barbican, must be careful that none of the perfect apples from the surface layer topple off and themselves are spoilt. Once he has left the uneven ground of the orchard, the way is mostly paved and he can dare to move more speedily. If there is any hope and resolve in his step, it is because each one he takes will bring him closer to Tabi in the outside world, for that is where he knows she is. She won't be hiding in a cellar or sulking in a cupboard or dislodging spirals of dust from the rafters of a pavilion. She will have taken on the wall.

On the far side of the gardens, after the sparrowgrass beds and the roots tubs, Ebon is surprised to see out of the corner of his eye the unmistakable scurrying of the angels' go-between. The man is heading, with some mighty purpose, through fallow fields which will be planted in the autumn with spring wheat and cabbages towards the geometric ranks of longbeam trees known as the lord's wilderness. Ebon is tempted to call out with a greeting as manners might dictate and as his obliging heart is prompting him. This can be another of his alms today: the gift of kindness when it's undeserved. He still feels that he has offended the man – and, therefore, his masters and their lord – by not acknowledging Alum's presence when he was burying the jack an afternoon ago. Here is a chance to make amends, even if it is with some-one who's broken women's fingers, and much worse. But something cautions him. Alum hurries like a man who does not want to be observed, and oddly he is not wear-ing his familiar grey-green cloak – his usual camouflage – and nor is he accompanied by his squeaking wheel. It isn't often that Alum is discovered, even on a fast-day afternoon, without his barrow close at hand. No, for the moment, Ebon hesitates and holds his peace.

Besides, what happens if he greets the man and, as is normal and polite, both of them draw near to each other and then pretend to be the best of neighbours and nei-ther angry with the other? Then Ebon's bound to put his basket down and Alum's bound to look inside. What alms are those? he'll want to know. What kind of beau-ties are you wasting there? Perhaps he'll step a little closer and, the practised snoop who never misses any clue, will see the juice of apple on Ebon's lips and smell the cooker on his breath and even spot a spat-out pip caught in the fabric of his smock. Then what? Rules broken on a fasting day, by a man already tainted by the company he's kept? The punishment could be severe. It isn't worth the greeting.

No, Ebon tries to look as if his load is far too heavy to notice anything or anyone other than the weight of his basket. He hurries on, head down, his eyes fixed on the ground ahead. After just a handful of paces, he dares to raise his eyes and witness the higher grasses and the rattle-weed shaking where the go-between has passed and disappeared so guiltily into the trees, the ring of unvisited woods and forbidding country, the out-of-bounds which have been planted to shield and distance the gardens and the farms from the estate's outer wall.

Ebon carries on with a greater skip to his step. His avoidance of Alum has made his load seem lighter or at least more manageable. Nevertheless, by the time he reaches the paved open courtyard which surrounds the barbican and its mighty gates to the world, his shoulder, his smock and the top of one trouser leg are soaked with sweat but mostly with apple juice. The soft and damaged fruit at the bottom has been cidered by the journey and has leaked through the basket's straw. Ebon is attracting flies. He'll need to wash and dry his clothes before another working day, but the communal tubs and lavers will all have been emptied out by now. He'll have to walk back to his bed and to his fasting-day supper of naught-from-the-larder and nothing-from-the-well by way of the stock pond. Tabi's chosen angel will doubtless let him wade in amongst the fish with his clothes on for a speedy scrubbing-down and, finally, a washing of his offending teeth and mouth. Then Ebon can stand in what remains of the evening light, a dripping penitent, and let the sun stiffen his wet clothes. His evening might be a slightly damp one, but, by dawn, they will be dry again and smelling more of pond and work than rotten fruit and sin.

By the time he has reached the upper entry to the courtyard and is being hailed by his brothers and his sisters, Ebon's step has lost its skip. He's not a man who normally is weakened by working long and hard. It's not his back or muscles that are aching. His spirit, though, is weary. It has been a heavy day – the solitude, the risks that he has taken, the rules he has offended, the sight of that man Alum doing who-knows-what-or-why, all in addition to the disquiet everyone has felt since Tabi left. If one thread loosens from the weave, all of it can fall apart.

He takes the final steps across the court and carefully lowers his basket to the ground at the table where the gatekeeper will sit and where, already, some of his fellow gardeners have brought their own largesses – overripe tomatoes, weeping sap into a trug, two huge and tough-skinned piglet marrows with dry-weather scars, bolted lettuce plants, podded peas and beans, a sack of what seems decent grain until the top is pulled aside and damper, rancid grain with the fine white tracery of mildew is revealed. There are also bags of bread from yesterday, some turnip shards and other kitchen waste. And clothes. A cold and hungry man might not refuse any of these gifts, but anyone with plenty on the table or cloth across their backs would rightly set these alms aside.

At least what Ebon has to offer on this fasting day of charity is larger and heavier than any of the other offerings. He turns the basket round a touch so that his gifts reflect the light. A single good apple topples to the ground and rolls away almost wilfully – a Tabi of the apple world, he thinks – so, on a whim, a rule breaker's whim, Ebon swings his arm and clods the wilful apple as fiercely as he can across the battlement into the hungry world beyond. He listens and he thinks he hears it landing. The gatekeeper steps out of his room and wags his finger in Ebon's face. He doesn't say a word but doesn't need to. His finger says that clodding apples over his high wall is not permissible. All alms must leave the garden by the gates. You throw an apple, his look implies, and what will happen next is apples thrown back. Or cores. Or curses. Even rocks. Throw an apple, get a stone, he means to say.

Ebon nods. He understands. But he is thrilled that he has sent with his own hands some alms into the world. He cannot help but imagine his sister waiting on the other side, her stomach empty and her orchard heart bereft, reaching up with her deft and practised hands — or, at least, the one that Alum hasn't snapped — to snatch the flying apple from the air. She's done as much before so many times. Catch this, Ebon has said, and sent a cooker sailing through the orchard, just a game, and she has stretched or reached or stooped to catch the apple crisply in her palm. This latest apple too is meant for her.

The keeper is the watchdog and the almoner. He is the only one allowed to draw back the bolts and pull open the gates for just as long as it takes for him to push the apple basket or any other alms that are being offered onto the slab of slate outside. He cannot use his hands, for fear of being brushed and tainted by death's cold fingertips, so he has two hazel stales to do the job, one flat-headed, to push the laden baskets out, and the other hooked, to retrieve the empty ones.

By now, the noisy group of onlookers and almsgivers — lord's witnesses, they call themselves — who have walked down to the barbican, all freshly washed and virtuous, has assembled as close as the sun and the gatekeeper will allow, wanting briefly to glimpse the outside world, that deepest mystery. A squint of life beyond their garden realms is all they're hoping for. And dreading. Especially today. They might have scrubbed themselves at the laver tubs but nothing has removed the dust of yesterday evening, the lord's own dust that rained down from his rafters and promised mayhem, tumult, danger, change.

The evening is still alive with heat and so most of the

witnesses have taken shelter in the shadow of the barbican's twin towers or underneath the row of ageing tarbonies which at this time, at the end of any working day, throw their shadows forward across the courtyard. Some of the witnesses, determined to be cheerful, clapped their hands and cheered when Ebon threw that single apple through the air. If the mood is briefly buoyant and expectant, it is only made more so by the restlessness since Tabi disappeared. Everyone is putting on their bravest faces to help them deal with the unhappy certainty that, tonight, they will be sharing their beds with empty stomachs and dry throats, and tomorrow . . . who amongst them dares to guess what tomorrows have in store? What once was counted on is now beyond their reckoning. One or two are tempted – especially when they spot those unusually fine apples at the top of Ebon's basket – to step out of the shade and walk the twenty paces to the timber gates, where, if the keeper would only turn away, an apple could be pocketed. As soon as midnight passes and the fasting day comes to an end, they'll pull their covers high to dampen out the noise of eating. They'll not want to have to share with anyone whom they've awoken by the crunch of that first bite. A secret apple in the muffled dark of fasting day is something to be enjoyed alone.

And yet a hollow stomach best befits the weekly giving of the alms. Their charity is deepened if they give food when – though only for a day – they have none to dine upon themselves. They put on their most solemn,

97

caring faces, keep their voices low, respect the custom of the gates by keeping out of sight of any worldly creature that might be outside waiting for the alms and looking in. They are allowed to sing the offertory or to applaud their own munificence when the gates are creaked apart. They can be heard but never seen.

Ebon turns away from the gates to join his sisters and his brothers in the shade and is surprised, when just a few steps have been taken, to be called back by the keeper. The apple basket is a problem, it would seem. The keeper is not muscular or toughened by his undemanding job. He has only to deal with bolts and hinges on fasting days but otherwise must just sit and watch, idling the time by swiping at a wasp or mammocking a butterfly – how very frail they are – and telling anyone who comes too close that they had better stay away or risk the taint of every-thing there is behind the wooden gates. He always takes great care himself, of course, to keep within the garden's bounds. He even washes down his hazel stales after each almsgiving and throws away the water that he uses and the rag for fear of their contagion. He is – like many men who are not rushed or overworked – a stickler for the rules.

However, this apple basket is too much for him alone. Not just the weight of it, not just the certainty that the fruit might topple to the ground as soon as it is lifted. He's spotted Ebon's back and thighs, how sticky wet they are with juice. The keeper likes to stay both clean and neat. So on this single occasion he will be a little flexible and have someone do the heavy work for him. He gestures at the orchardman to stay exactly where he is, in the shadow of the gates, until commanded to step forward and, with his practised muscles, propel the alms into the world.

Ebon does what he is told, unnerved a little but honoured too. He knows of no one else who's had the chance to witness an almsgiving from such close quarters. He is uneasy, though. He knows the risks. He knows the rules. He can be heard but never seen. He stands and watches. He is tense. A cloud of midges is brought out of hiding by the offerings of food and by the chance of dining out on the apple juice soaked into Ebon's smock. He'd brush them off but does not want to draw attention to himself.

There is a ritual to observe. The keeper dons his yellow cap and cape and so becomes the almoner. He takes his great handbell, with its polished, hardwood handle, its decorated waist and inscription bands, steadies the clapper for a moment and then lets ring. He is a practised hand with it. The strikes are even, fast and sinuous. Their music is both jubilant and startling. The rooster rooks in the tarbonies are disturbed and take flight but only for a few short wheels. If they caw, they can't be heard above the clappering. Even Ebon's flies pause in their feasting as they sense the quavers of the bell.

The almoner deadens the brass with his hand. The silence is almost as startling as the ringing itself. Now

99

everybody underneath the trees is concentrating on the gates. The handbell will have sounded just the same for any hungry fellows waiting on the far side of the barbican. They too will no doubt be waiting with bated breath for the weekly crack of light as the timbers open up and, for a moment, eden and the world can share and breathe a common air.

The almoner has dripped a little pine oil on the four heavy bolts and so they slip back readily when he pushes against their slides and make a satisfying ding. Now he lifts his chin to summon Ebon. He might as well make good use of the man and let him lift the two heavy timber beams that keep the gates secure. All that remains is to tug gently at the rope handles and pull the two gates inwards just wide enough to make passage for the alms.

Ebon is fearful and has to back away, to gasp even, when the laden breeze outside strikes his cheeks and forehead, as damp as fever. The almoner does not bother to conceal his lofty smile. He is as used to fevered air as Ebon is to apples. Of all the garden's habitants, he is the one who earns his supper and his bed from working – sitting is the truer word – closest to the outside world. He is its familiar and has been now for . . . well, some numbers are too great to count. But he has not forgotten those first fasting days, when furloughed from more heavy duties with a hoe and spade because of his small size – he's not half as lofty as his self-regard – he had to pull the great gates back and offer their oblations to the world. Those were happier times, with less hunger and dismay outside, he thinks. The baskets of fruit and produce and the bags of staling bread were sometimes left untouched until the morning and then not seized on as greedily as they are nowadays or squabbled over. But, even so, he was as fearful then as Ebon, he supposes, is today of sharing air with them and has himself stepped back with that same nervous gasp. No wonder, though. How many times they've both been told and still are told in sermons and in readings that the mortals, dwellers all in time and space, exist on foul and paltry air. They have their ration of it. So many lungfuls each. Then no more. Each meagre breath of it is weary with the weight of days.

Ebon knows the meaning of that smile. He is being very gently mocked for his timidity. So he steps forward once again and stands almost at the gatekeeper's shoulder, close enough at least to smell the pine oil on the bolts. The keeper means to test him now. He reaches for the stouter of the two hazel stales and passes it to the orchardman. Down on your knees, he says. And shove.

It is not a difficult task for anyone as strong and flexible as Ebon. He pushes out the bags of bread and porridge grain first, making sure to do so blindly, neither being seen nor seeing, and then the lighter wraps and ties of green leaves and beans which have bulk but little weight to them. Then there are curds, candies, rinds and honeycomb, more rancid than they ought to be, wrapped in dock and barley straw. Their passing out obscures even the smell of pine oil for a moment. Next are potatoes and the heavy roots, distorted ones, or those severed by a careless spade, or greening from being left too long in light. Then tomatoes, overripe and pungent, their punnet stained red with juice.

Ebon leaves his apples to the very last. He is, it must be said again, ashamed of them, at least he is ashamed of what those people waiting at the gates will discover when they remove that deceiving layer of hand-picked fruit and find the mushy windfalls underneath. His alms are a pittance, mostly — that's to say, a gift that's mean and pitiful, for pity's sake.

He is slow and cautious with his basket. Taking care down on his knees at the scarcely open gates, with the tiny keeper looking on, is not a simple task. Maintaining his balance, without both hands to steady him, is a challenge. As is acting blindly, as instructed. Alms should be offered with all modesty, with lowered eyes, bowed head, proudly and invisibly.

Again — a third time in the day — he breaks a rule and lifts his head and looks out on the world, for there might be a face to recognize. He is surprised how normal it all is, how similar to what he knows on his side of the gates. The outer timbers and the stonework of the wall must look the same from wherever they are viewed. The wooden bridge, which crosses a dry moat to connect the barbican to the flatlands beyond, is exactly like the bridges he has crossed inside the lord's estate. The distances seem greater, though, as does the sky's vast depth and height. But there is light and there are clouds and there is birdsong. Even the domes and ramparts of far-off forests remind him of the orchards where he works. He cannot help but wonder if he has been told a pack of lies, that death is just a story that the angels tell, to keep their servants trapped and tame, exactly as his Tabi had foretold.

There is the clattering of feet on earth and then resoundingly on wood. He sees them first: bare or ill-shod, unclean. And then he lifts his chin to witness the flock of hungry scavengers closing in on that day's offerings, like geese or pigs contending for the kitchen scraps. His view of them is too brief for detail. There is a moment, just a shard of time and light, in which he might have got back on his feet and in a step or two squeezed through the gates to join them at the feast and then to carry on to find his Tabi in the greater world. But his chance is missed before it truly crosses his mind. It is only later that he can imagine it. He sees himself, a giant amongst the scavengers, unhesitating and resolved. But in that moment, the keeper pulls the stale backwards out of his grip and, barely missing Ebon's hands as he steadies himself on the ground, steps forward to slam shut the great gates with all the force he can muster. Their impact can be heard by everybody watching underneath the tarbonies.

Ebon is asked by all those witnesses and neighbours

what he saw in those moments when he glimpsed the world. He gives an honest answer but does not share it all. He says, You'd not mistake them for ourselves. Some faces looked as gnarled and weathered as an oak; others were more grey and blistered. And you'd be shocked by them, he says. He is used to a sheen and smoothness of the skin, what an orchardman would count as plumpness in an apple, readiness. But here were faces that were over-ripened, wrinkled, softened, blemished, blossomed pale with mould and thin. And there were young ones, children he supposes, half the size of anybody in the garden, even the almoner. They were bewildering, he says. They looked as helpless as the angels, clumsy and dependent. And there were rags for clothes and bones for arms and heads that couldn't boast a single hair, and others that were white, and others that looked as long and lustreless as grotto weed. Say more, tell more, they beg. But he does not want to add the one thing that has shocked him most. He feels that he's encountered animals.

8

IF ALUM MEANS to satisfy his masters with some useful intelligence about their absent hand – and save his own skin – he must now trespass on the garden's margins, where the great stone outer defences and the inner palisades of sharpened stakes are a warning to all the brothers and the sisters to keep away. Go close and you might taste the tainted and contagious air of the world beyond, they are warned with unrelenting frequency. The wall, except at the barbican, is out of bounds and should not be offended by so much as the dab of a fingertip. But even getting close is tricky.

Viewed and flattened from above, the lord's estate is a perfect circle. More than a circle, so the angels say. It's designed to be a wheel with rigid pathways for spokes and a flinted limestone battlement for its rim. The garden's geometric nave, its hub, its heart, is where the greatest order can be found. Buildings must have corners and straight lines. Prayer rooms, belfries and pavilions might be fanciful, but they must be stable too. Without it they might fall. Even when the buildings have been left behind for the working day and the habitants, busy with their tasks, walk down the footways and the pavements into the nearest cloistered gardens and the salad beds, they will still encounter only tidiness and harmony – and, if they don't, if an edging stone, perhaps, has been knocked out of true or if some weed has dared to spring a leaf or the root-run of a bush has broken surface, it's their duty to stoop down and fix it there and then. Order is the order of the day.

Even further out from the nave, amongst the orchards, the enclosures and the fields, where nature is allowed a greater say, the husbandry is inflexibly imposed. There's satisfaction to be found in that. The hedges are kept trim, the fences in repair, the furrow lines as straight and pleasing as any beam, the plantings balanced and designed. But the lord's control is more pliantly imposed in the deep ring of undergrowth and trees which shields the land that provides for the table from the garden's boundary wall. There, the country loses shape. It was planted formally an age ago with a serried host of dark-leaved lookalikes, tidy longbeams of equal height and matching span, but since has been allowed to defy the lord's designs and become unruly and unkempt, a tangle and a barrier of fallen limbs and snagging roots, together with a thicketing of anything the birds or winds bring in: brambles, ivys, bracken, rattleweed and brush. The angels keep it so, they say, to filter out the deadly air of the world. Gardeners are never sent with hatchets or rakes to tidy up or fell. Nobody, other than those with disloyalty in mind, would even try to penetrate these forbidding and forbidden outer margins of the lord's estate.

Yet, on this troubled fasting afternoon, when his absence from any supper table will not be noticed, Alum means to shoulder through and reach the wall. He's looking out for signs of an escape, a broken branch, perhaps, a displaced piece of stone where Tabi might have pressed a foot, a discarded length of rope, a snag of cloth, some evidence of haste or climbing. He is excited, actually. Not only is there a mystery to solve, there's also the chance of a recapture. He has her by her fingers once again.

He will not wear his cloak for this adventure. It is too fine. It could catch on brambles and on thorns when he's obliged to force his way through undergrowth. He puts the moleskin purse with its polished stones at the bottom of his trug, folds and lays the cloak on top, then places them all in the deep end of his barrow. That'll have to stay behind as well. It's far too wide and clumsy for what he has in mind. Besides, he does not want the squeaking wheel to draw attention to his doings. He pushes it, with its treasured contents, into thick shrubbery at the far side of the spring wheat and cabbage field, though within sight of the path that leads down to the barbican. He stands back and checks from several angles to satisfy himself it can't be seen and touched by any passer-by. He feels bereft already, stripped bare even, by this brief parting. He sometimes wonders if the only things he dares to love and trust are those he has made himself. The barrow's squeak has been his make-do friend.

There is a single figure on the path. It's hard for Alum to tell at first who it might be, apart from that it is a man, his face half turned to the side. But the apples are a give-away, in every sense. It's the orchardman with a basket of alms on his shoulder and hardly managing the weight. The last thing Alum wants is a conversation. He does not think he – or his barrow – has been seen, but neverthe-less he ducks and hurries off. In twenty stooping steps he's out of sight entirely, hidden amongst the longbeam trunks. Then with both foreboding and elation he heads towards the wall.

He has begun his journey in a part of the lord's wil-derness where he knows the canopy is dense and the undergrowth, shielded from the sun and rain, will be at its sparsest, and the earth firm. It's gloomy, but the going is easy, and there are clearings where the light breaks through and where he can stop to draw breath, check the treetops just in case the woman is hiding there, up to her squirrel tricks, and calculate from how the sunbeams play between the branches which direction he should take next. His step is springy, eager even, purposeful, despite his sleepless night and the burden of his respon-sibilities. Today he feels less lonely than usual, though he is entirely on his own. He is discovering what the woman he's hunting for has always known, that trees are company. They ease and sigh and mutter as he hurries past, replying to the leafy chatter of his feet as he seeks out a path.

Before long he can hear the wall itself or, at least, he can hear the mayhem of the outside world buffeting its masonry and seeming to murmur its repeated warning not to touch. A steady, satisfying breeze shifts the topmost twigs and looser branches of the trees. They bend and give, obligingly. But the sound of wind on wall is something unfamiliar. It's stubborn and implacable. The wind complains about the stone; the stone ignores the wind.

It is a relief to reach more sunlit ground. Beyond the palisade of sharpened stakes at which he must narrow his shoulders, like a cat, to squeeze between, it rises to a ridge, muscly with boulders. He climbs it, swivels for the view along the garden's boundaries, and sits down on a rock for a moment to take stock and regain his breath. From this rise, the wall seems lower than he's imagined it – it is eclipsed by trees – but, even in its modesty, is sacred and implacable. It has the added height and weight of never being touched. Each block of stone declares itself as upright, virtuous and innocent. For the moment, Alum dares not step too close. He does not even want to desecrate its shadow. But he can follow it. In which direction, though? It really makes no difference. The garden is encircled by the wall. What's left behind will lie ahead whichever way he goes. Alum is almost blinded by the brightness after the day-dusk of the canopy, and so he turns his back against the sun and with a leaping heart goes widdershins along the ridge. With the light behind him, he can best discover Tabi's spoors and traces.

There is a path of sorts which, Alum supposes, has been worn by animals. It is by turn rocky, marshy, snagged by bushes, heavy on the feet and treacherous. He's panting, but he hardly dares to breathe too deeply. He imagines he can taste and smell the world's contagious gases beyond the thickness of the wall, which is in places bright with flint and in others damp and mossy but always grim and daunting. So Alum does not part his lips if he can help it but rather inhales through his nostrils, shallowly. Too shallowly. He is already feeling faint. He is not used to such exertions in such heat. The way would be challenging for anyone whose everyday life, like the go-between's, is effortless. At this time of the afternoon, he'd most expect to be resting in the shade with his back against a trunk. But he presses on. He will not rest again until he has put out of sight the regiments of planted trees and has found that low and dipping part of the wall where by all reports it's easiest to clamber up. Indeed, it's where Jamin, the feeble angel, the stink-fish master who is despised even by his fellows, plunged and injured his wing – or pretended to. Alum has decided that the angel is a perjurer and fraud, a feckless, crafty enemy of eden, who can fly if he says he can't and can't fly if he claims he can.

In Alum's brief experience – he's only ventured this way, say, twice before and both times in pursuit of miscreants – this is the one section in the whole, circular length of the wall where a body, small as Tabi's, can hope to reach the top and get away. There the animal track which skirts the boundary is at its darkest and most over-grown, and conveniently is very nearly out of sight of the wall's great heaven-pointing towers at the barbican, which is just a furlong further down the track. Nobody has a proper reason to be so far from fields and gardens. Any disturbance not caused by animals must therefore count as a suspicious sign.

Alum walks more slowly now, on tiptoe almost, because it is there – where the narrowing path, together with its companion wall and the inner fringe of planted oaks, dips low to cross a gully – that he imagines the tabitha's escape took place. She will, no doubt, have lis-tened many times to her playmate Jamin's self-pitying account of where and how he snapped his foolish wing and then collided with the masonry. The sister would have known through her collusions with that fallen angel where she might find an easy way to scale the wall, to grip it with her sinful hands.

So Alum pauses, turns on his heel, searching for a way of escape through the undergrowth. It's only when he goes down on his knees that he discovers a passage.

There's hardly any path, in fact, but just a squeeze for animals through nettles and thorns. The thickets there might well conspire to place defectors out of sight, but they also make defectors pay a bloody price. He has to crawl through undergrowth for what, if he were standing up, would be just twenty steps before he reaches the stony foot of the rampart, with tussock grass and beds of scarlet mallows. Some of the estate's more lofty trees – they'd benefit from lopping, surely, he might suggest – have stretched their boughs across into the world. Some snags of ivy have come loose, and vines are swinging above his head, just within reach for someone of his height, though he has to jump to get a decent grip. This must be it, Alum tells himself, wanting to believe. This is where the woman has climbed. She hasn't had to desecrate the wall. He'll try to follow her, until . . . until he dare not take a further step.

He clutches the ivy snags with both hands, surprised to find how tough and sinewy they are and thrilled to be, at last, this daring, unseen version of himself. They swing and sink under his weight but he perseveres. It takes him three attempts but finally he manages to pull himself up into the split of a tree trunk and then to gain the crotch of three wide branches. It's safe and solid there, though the height is alarming. The looking-down is harder than the looking-up, he's found. He can't imagine ever getting down to earth again. Now he allows himself to rest and make a plan. A little higher up the tree the greatest and the flattest of the boughs yearns out across the boundary wall, a wooden bridge and footpath into the world for anyone who's used to climbing trees. Alum is a calculating, careful man. He schemes ahead. He sees which higher branches will provide hand-holds and where his feet will safely fit. Three limbs bracing, one limb stretching, that's his nervous strategy. For a moment he imagines that the bough gives way and he tumbles through the air and bounces off the outer wall as Jamin almost did. That fool. He's pinned down by all the debris of the tree which has split and fallen after him. He cannot move. A broken ankle's not the best way to begin a new life in the world of time. Then it is night, and he is barking like a fox for help.

It is only once he's satisfied he's capable that Alum, with great care and even greater trepidation, takes his first step on the bough. For all he's claimed that he has almost sprouted wings, in all of his eternity he's never been so far from earth before. He takes half-steps, a shuffle rather than a stride. The bough sags and shudders with his every move. He shakes and tests the smaller branches before he grips them to secure himself. His hands are trembling but he is determined too.

Although it seems an age, it really isn't very long before Alum can, by clinging on and leaning out, push his face beyond the veil of leaves and look down on the flinty summit of the wall. For the first time in his endless life, he smells the salt and sugar of the outside world. So now he's partly satisfied. Tabi isn't captured yet but at least he has found and proved a route that she might have used for her escape. She must have stood where he is standing now. She must have gripped the self-same branches he has held. She'd simply have to drop from the bough onto the masonry – a distance that is only as far as she is tall – and then . . . well, then, if her knees and ankles survived the impact and her soul survived the sin, she'd either have to climb down smooth stone to put her foot onto the world, or fly. Unless she had a rope.

Alum looks around but sees no sign of any rope or of any scar where it might have been secured. There's not so much as a broken twig or the scuff of a shoe to prove that she was ever there, though there are disturbances, the kind of talon marks that might be caused by birds. Or angels. But he senses her, her residue, her scent. He cocks his head and flares his nostrils. He fancies that he smells again what he detected in the empty dormitory this morning as he knelt by Tabi's bed. Her body, on the coverlets and pillows. He has all that he was hoping for, a story for the angels. He reaches up and snaps some twigs. He scuffs the bough with his shoes, dislodging pieces of bark which fall onto the ground beneath the tree at the base of the wall. Perhaps he should have brought some of her clothes from the pile next to her bed, he thinks. One of her headscarves hanging from a branch? Well, that would settle it.

But Alum really does not need more evidence of Tabi's

flight. He only has to place her on the bough and he has proof to satisfy his masters. He isn't fool or heretic enough to drop down onto the sacred summit of the wall himself to test if it is possible. The distance is too great and his daring is too slight. Besides, if he swings down to test his suspicions, he'll not be able to swing up again and tell his tale this evening. Dropping is the easy part — and Tabi would have managed it without a moment's fear. He winces at the thought of it. How his own ankles would crack and how his ribcage would ram into his teeth if he were to do the same.

No, she'd not have any need for rope, as he's first suspected. Or to sprout wings. Tabi's lithe and light enough to drop from heights, he thinks, and land as safely as a cat. She does that sort of thing anyway, for work. The orchard-woman can reach and pick the highest fruit by hand, and prune and lop and pollard amongst the uppermost branches. She must have jumped from a bough onto grasses a thousand times and never hurt herself. The angels will assent to that. They've seen her working; they have seen it from above. They know she's willowy and supple. They know she's like an angel, unafraid of heights, that even dropping from the wall into the moat below is not beyond her skills. What does he recommend, they'll want to know, to prevent a further disobedience from anyone, like Tabi, who's used to climbing, jumping, dropping? Cut back the swags of ivy, he will say. Burn out the brush and undergrowth. Take saws and amputate the yearning bough. Lock up or tether anyone who might wish to follow her. Lock up anyone who must have helped her to get away, some willing brother with wide shoulders and strong arms who could readily have lifted her onto the ivy swags.

Even though it has been several days since she's gone missing, Alum — still balancing amidst the branches of the tree — calls her name, just in case she remains within hearing. There is no answer to his calling out — but he dares to edge a little further along the bough until it is springy and unstable. At last he peers, with trembling nervousness, onto the forbidden ground below and then out into the world. It is the first time he's transgressed like this. Yet nothing is remarkable. It's only eden amplified. The horizon is so remotely distant that Alum's eyes cannot define it clearly. There is no wall beyond this wall, as far as he can tell. Their land must open out eternally. The view is limitless, just undulations, greys and greens, a sky so wide it seems impossible, disrespectful even, vast. His body shudders with a gripping chill. He steps back in alarm. The size and distance are too great to contemplate.

He moves away, half fainting from the fright. The canopy of leaves closes once more around him, and, with their waking sweep across his face, he feels alarm again but for a different reason. Is feeling just a little faint the first sign of a sleep that never ends? Has his nose-tip breached the air beyond the garden of the lord? he wonders. Has his pecked skin advanced too far? Has he risked, unknowingly, a toe? He half expects to feel death's teeth sink in at once, for death, if it exists, is bound to hunt with fangs. He even looks down at his feet, where he might very well discover mangled shoes and two sets of bloody toes. He might have killed himself, he thinks, by daring to stand so close to death, by having squandered his eternity with just the thickness of his skin. It has been tantalizing to glimpse and whiff forbidden land, how wide it is and deep, and how it tastes, but he will not sleep tonight for fear of never waking up.

It is only when he twists around and steadies himself on the bough to face the tree's great trunk and begin his journey home that Alum catches sight again of the jar-walled towers at the barbican gates and the familiar pair of slanting roofs, below which he can easily imagine the almsgivers on this, a fasting day. He is hardly surprised, then, when he sees what must be an apple or potato sailing through the air, thrown by a strong arm from the courtyard by the barbican. Alum has witnessed almost everybody at one time or another flinging produce, sticks or stones over the battlement just to feel they've made a mark outside. All those hopeful lobbers want is some response, some cry perhaps, some distant thud, or even something thrown back by way of thanks. Then, when there's nothing – there is always nothing – they must shrug and turn away, though they often seem more light-hearted than before, and more fully shriven of their troubles. Whatever has been thrown out into the world has unburdened them.

Again, he leans a little further out to see the missile – yes, it's an apple – tumble to the ground and in plain sight. Here's something else he can report as soon as he gets back to the angels' loft. The orchardman has thrown it, he's sure – Who else has fruit like that on fasting days? – and for a purpose that is obvious. Alum tells a story to himself in which the orchard-woman, the escapee, has caught the apple in her hand or stopped it rolling with her foot and now is sitting with her skirts tucked up above her knees and eating it, still dining out on free food from the garden just as she has suppered, far too many times, on stolen food. He can recall her pippy face, slimy with juice the day he caught her literally red-handed. It was more than a pleasure to seize her by her wrists and twist her fingers back against the bone until she let go. He'd rarely been so close to her. But there she was, her fingers almost snapping in his hands, her breath and his breath buffeting. He can imagine jumping down into the world and taking hold of her again today, before she has a chance even to raise this orchard-windfall to her mouth. He'll have her sinking to the ground, her free hand slapping at his thighs, until the apple's rolling loose again, and order is restored.

His reverie is ended by the clang of the almoner's handbell and, not long after, by the cries of people from the outside world, running from their fields and huts or wherever they have work and dwellings towards the gatehouse bridge, where soon, as is usual on fasting days, the gifts of food will be shunted out by invisible hands. A landscape that was empty of any living thing is now busy with the poor of spirit and of wealth racing for their suppers.

It is not Tabi but a slow and ancient man – doubtless used to getting to the gates too late for anything but scraps – who discovers Ebon's clodded apple. He does not eat it there and then, but examines it and looks about him for a fitting tree from which it must have fallen and where there should be more. But there are no apple trees. He shakes his head – such are the wonders of the world, he must be thinking – and in doing so catches sight of Alum in his leafy hiding place, high above the summit of the wall. The old man shakes a bony fist at his observer, and it would seem he half considers throwing the apple at him too. But, instead, with impressive speed and dexterity for such an ancient, he scoops up a palmful of stones from the ground and sends them clattering against the sacred masonry.

Alum scrambles down as quickly as he can, breaking ivy, snagging bark. He'll report to the angels, telling them that he has found proof of Tabi's flight, that he knows how she got away, and that there is evidence: the disturbed ivy and the bruised bark, the marks of climbing and snapped twigs. Give me time, he'll say, and I will discover who it was that let that sister get away so easily.

That man – he will not name the fellow straight away – is bound to want to follow her. And when that happens, Alum means to be both the witness and the judge, quick to seize him by the ankle or the wrist, mid-flight, with his firm hand, and so save him from the world and death – and so save himself. Ebon, Ebon the fruit-picker, the darling of the trees, caught in the act of disobedience, and the angels' go-between rewarded for his diligence.

It is almost dusk when Alum regains the spring fields and the cultivated cloisters of the estate. He is not being careful any more. The semi-darkness cloaks him, he believes. But, once he reaches the open ground and the shrubbery where he has hidden his cloak, his barrow and his tools, he can see the group of habitants returning from the almsgiving, cheerful and chattering amongst themselves, despite the prospects of a supperless evening. Last in line are the orchardman himself, an empty basket limp at his shoulder, and the gatekeeper, trailing him a few steps back like a loyal dog and still dressed as the yellow almoner.

Alum waits amongst the longbeam trunks until the path is entirely clear of walkers and then hurries over to his barrow. It's upside down. It has been widdershinned. The wooden axle of the squeaky wheel is snapped, by force. The trug is underneath the barrow's upturned body, almost flattened. All the laths are splintered. What remains is hardly bulkier than the leaf litter on the ground. It is as if some mighty wind – mean and personal – has tossed his handiworks against a rock or some great foot has stamped on them, made heavier by anger, or as if – a common phrase – the heavens themselves have descended and pitted their great weight against the world. His fragile hand-made innocents are silenced and abused. Misfortunes come in threes, it's said in recent days. But why not dozens? he asks himself. Why not scores? What else will end up in pieces and in splinters, now that smashing up has found a place in eden? There'll be confusion worse confounded, as the angels say, with ruin upon ruin, and rout on rout, if there's no longer order in their gardens and their fields. These shards of wood are warning him that eden and its votaries are now more fragile than he'd thought possible.

Alum's cry of distress is shrill and piercing, too thinly sharp perhaps to reach the ears of those departing almsgivers. The hatred cripples him. He kneels, as he might do in prayer, to see how bad the damage is to his barrow. Well, it has proved strong enough to keep its shape, but its linings have been smashed and the wheel and axle are detached. The trug is useless now. He is at once resigned to that, though not resigned to his own injured pride or his wounded heart. He cannot stop himself from adding his own weight in a wanton spasm to the task of flattening it completely. He stamps on it until it is reduced to little more than tinder. He'll not be outdone, especially by an enemy. His feet and nobody else's

121

will have the final say. And later, in the lord's good time, revenge will sweeten his dismay.

At last, he finds his cloak, ripped and muddied and flung into a bush. His moleskin purse is gaping open below it. The polished gemstones with which he's planned to purchase company are emptied out onto the ground and scattered by a foot as if they are as worthless as plum pits. He grinds a couple with his heel into the ground. Let the crows and magpies play with them. But then, in time – the time is takes for tears to spill and then to dry – he comes back coldly, damply, to his senses. The purse and stones are stolen goods and valuable. It's best to keep them hidden. So again – but with a shaking hand – he gathers up each glinting piece and hides them under his cloak.

Alum has to hug his chest to calm himself. He knows precisely who to blame. His rival and his enemy, the orchardman, was walking on the path when Alum hid his tools and treasures. He must have noticed it and, being cunning – you cannot trust a smiling man – waited until the angel's go-between disappeared into the woods, before stepping boldly across the field to the shrubbery and exacting his revenge. What Alum doesn't notice, though – the day is drawing to a close, becoming dark and secretive – is something bluer than the bluest of the stones: one short feather from a wing, shaken loose and caught amongst the smithered wood. There's been an angel there today.

9

JAMIN IS FEARFUL of a visitor. His two helpers and their hunger have already been given leave by bells to go back to their beds. They have been slugs all morning as if fasting were a penance rather than a devotion to be savoured. Nobody's at their best when all they have for nourishment is air. But still the stock-pond angel would prefer to keep their company and tolerate their idleness and their surliness than be alone. If they were to tarry until dusk, they could be his witnesses – and his protectors, possibly – when Alum comes, as he is bound to do.

Now that he is alone, though, and not distracted by any duties, Jamin has little else to busy him but dread of the battle that must lie ahead. The version that he tells himself – in which his standing as an angel is all the protection he needs and in which his exalted, feathered rank renders him untouchable – does not persuade for very long. It seems more likely that the go-between will come squalling down the pathway to the pondside armed with the largest and the heaviest piece of shattered barrow he can find. Then, driven on by that choler only men possess and the certainty that none of his other, grander masters really care if Jamin flies again or not, he will set about his adversary's one good wing. A man who'll snap a woman's fingers to pay for a tomato surely will not hesitate to charge a greater price for what has happened to his handiworks. There'll be a blow for every broken lath and spoke, and each one laden with a curse. *And I deserve it,* Jamin cannot help but think. *What kind of angel am I now? It was spiteful to destroy the barrow and the trug. The man's entitled to his rage.*

It's wise, if cowardly, for Jamin to put himself in a safer place before the retribution catches up with him. He is not fond of water – despite or, maybe, because of his angelic duties there – and he abhors the pond's putrid stink, especially when the mires are disturbed by anybody wading in. He's often nursed an image of himself, on idle and more lonely days, in which he's floating face down – held down – in the shallows, drowning till the end of time. Nevertheless, he launches himself from his raised bower and manages to clear the pond with a painless if ungainly flight and land amongst the reeds, cattails and teasels on the far side. There, if he stays still and does not sneeze, he can keep watch and not be seen. He has been feeling faint-hearted all afternoon, sapped of energy not only by his fast – though angels are supposed to be like birds and capable of flying on empty stomachs for several days on end – but by remorse. He has committed the mighty sin of vengefulness and that is tiring. Not just the shame of it but all the effort it has taken too. You are an angel, he told himself at the time, when Alum's handiworks lay shattered at his feet, and can exact whatever punishments you want. But how he wishes now that he had not let his feelings take control, when, just by chance that afternoon, while testing his bad wing in flight for the first time in a month of moons, he caught sight of Alum, heading off . . . well, who knows where? . . . into the lord's wilderness but leaving his infuriating barrow hidden in a thicket of shrubbery. It was, at first, more impishness than malice that made Jamin flap across to look. He didn't plan to take the thing apart, just to give vent. Once he'd started, though, and exerted just a little pressure on the handle of the barrow and listened to it crack and split, there was no stopping him.

It wasn't easy work. But he persisted, in a righteous spasm, unable to prevent himself. For some wild moments, he was like a woodhawk silencing a squab, coming down upon the body of Alum's barrow time after time, until eventually the slats and the narrow axle, together with its squeak, proved too flimsy and too weakly built to withstand the angel's beak and weight. The wrecking of the trug was a petty afterthought, and even less forgivable. What had it ever done but carry food from stem to plate? He had only to stamp on it the once to prove how vengeful he could be.

It was just as well that, as he fled the pile of splintered wood, Jamin spotted – and scattered with a kick – the purse of polished gemstones that Alum had left hidden. At least he could now persuade himself, if fleetingly, that he was guilty not of malice but only of rewarding Alum for his thieving ways as one might, say, reward a worker for the filching of tomatoes. Ah, yes, tomatoes! They were the juicy, nagging symbols of the truth. His appalling ruthlessness was not because of stolen stones, or the ever-squeaking wheel, or even the betrayals of the past and the treacheries to come, but because of the orchard-woman. Tabi was the grit in his eye as he bore down on Alum's implements. If he was being pitiless, he was being so for her.

Jamin is still washing off his shame and guilt when his visitor arrives. His belly is deep in the shallows of the pond and he is rinsing out his mouth, eye to eye with a couple of the stock fish that have risen to the bait of his familiar face. He is doing his best to observe the spirit of the fast – which he has already tainted with his violence and anger – by not swallowing any water, weed or floating seed, when he hears the expected crash of someone breasting through the undergrowth, coming not from the estate's cluster of buildings, as he has anticipated, but from the other side, the outer side. He ducks below the screen of rushes and teasels, instinctively. And he prepares himself. He has practised sentences which he can offer in his own defence. He has rarely known such fear or felt more foolish. What has become of him? He is the sodden angel in the reeds, the craven master of the fish, cowering as if he were the lowliest of men, besotted with a woman. Indeed, he even wants it to be true. How often he has longed to have the body and the essence of a man, and how just as frequently, he must suppose, the go-between has prayed to be equipped with wings. The lord must have mixed them up when they were made and mistaken plumes for skin. Well, let there be a restitution, then, a putting right of that mistake. Jamin will swap his roost in the night-time loft for Alum's place at the table. He'll eat with Tabi at his side, then share the bedside air with her in sleep. If only wings were arms. If only there were miracles.

Again, there is a crashing in the undergrowth. Who-ever is approaching is quite near but in no hurry by the sound of it. There is no fury in his step, certainly not enough to be Alum's. But it's not an angel, clearly. Jamin's feathered fellows are announced more artfully, by just a flash of blue, a hastening shadow and a rustle of plumage when they descend on him, once in a while, to pry or even wash their feathers as he is doing now. Their com-pany is as unlikely as it is unwelcome. It's not preceded by the pushing back of branches and the snapping underfoot of twigs.

What Jamin still fears to see is Alum's broad and brutal face, looming at him through the reeds, his make-shift weapon raised, his feet already splashing in the pond. He's never before heard a tale in which a habitant has dared to strike an angel, but anything can happen once, he must suppose. Besides, who would truly blame the man if, bereaved of those essential tools he's fashioned for himself, he would seek to revenge himself and not simply – and in keeping with the scriptures – let the judgement be the lord's? Jamin remembers all too well that evening when he sat with Tabi at the table in the refectory and was fool enough to let them feed him from their plates as if he were a chicken or a cat. He could imagine for a while that he was their dear and trusted friend. He ruffles at the memory. He had to hurry after Alum and beg him not to carry word of it to any of the greater angels. And if I do? the go-between asked. And Jamin, a fearful quaver in his voice, only offered in reply the usual formula when angel is annoyed by man: The heavens will descend on you. And so the heavens are descending now, on me, he thinks. The go-between will be inflamed and dangerous. The fish might gorge themselves tonight on blood.

It is a jolt, both welcome and surprising, to see his visitor is not the go-between. It's Ebon at the far side of the pond. There's no mistaking his dark head or his muscled height. He must weigh twice as much as idle Alum ever will. Jamin likes the orchardman, though their paths hardly cross. Ebon never sickens, never needs a restful day, so has not been consigned to work with Jamin at the stock pond, where a friendship might be forged. And

Jamin rarely — or hardly ever since he smashed his wing — flies down to the orchard or the nuttery. It's not his business to be there and will not be until his fish decide to roost in trees. No, he likes Ebon on a whim. Who doesn't like a well-set man who smiles? Besides, they are heart brothers, though in very different ways, the one a soulmate and a friend, the other just a foolish supplicant. Yet both claim Tabi as an intimate and both are grieving for her loss.

Ebon splashes in, his clothes still on his back and hips. He flounders in the pond, unsteadied by the heaviness of water, the unexpected depth, the unexpected smell, and the unstable mire up to his ankles. No one in eden ever learnt to swim. No fish are rising for this flailing bait. His arrival has been sudden and shocking for them, far worse than any heron's. They all are hiding in the greater depths and under blanket weed and lily pads, ancestrally expecting someone with a pan or net to scoop them out for cooking. Now that Ebon has secured his footing in the mud, he ducks beneath the surface, to wash off any trace of apple juice even from his hair. He rubs his clothes, submerges once again and surfaces, his tunic dark with water. He only wades ashore more heavily than he waded in once he has brushed off all the gripweed and a snail and any residue of death that he has picked up on his hands, down at the barbican.

Ebon checks the chevet sky. It is already purple-grey. Even the western horizons are sombering. There's not sufficient heat in the sun and not enough daylight left to dry his clothes this evening without some help. He strips them off and stands as spotless, gleaming, and naked as a shelled filbert on the pond's bank, swinging his sodden clothes around his head as if he means to let them fly, while much of the water in them is loosened into the air. He needs a good flat rock on which to beat them dry. He looks for one, and it is only now that he spots the angel hiding, still as a heron, blue as a dragonfly, his plumage almost blending with a clump of irises beyond the reeds. They bow their heads in greeting, clearly not alarmed to have each other's company – but self-conscious too.

Ebon looks down at Jamin in the pond and at his damaged but still glossy wing angled awkwardly away from his flanks. What a blessing it must be to be able to sink yourself in water and then, with the merest shiver and a flick, be dry again. Feathers are more practical than smocks and trousers, hats and shoes. They resist the water with their oils. What a wondrous benison it must be to be created plumed like that, to be an angel fully fledged, while he – Ebon looks down on his naked self – must live and labour wrapped in threads or else die from cold at night and burn by day. He swirls his clothes a few times more around his head, with greater recklessness and speed than before, and this time lets them fly as he cannot himself. It's irresistible. He will be rid of them, if only for a moment.

The orchardman's clothes thud into the deep grasses

just a few steps away. His gesture has been comically absurd. He cries out happily and spreads his arms. A whoop of celebration for the day. He's still alive and there is hope. He's glimpsed the world and those who starve in it. He does not dread it any more.

Jamin is thinking he's the clumsy, foolish one, caught hiding in the reeds and rushes like some deceitful coot. The orchardman does not seem the least absurd to him at all, but just happily exuberant in ways that angels never can. If Ebon's envious of an angel's feathers, Jamin wishes he could be the dripping, naked one, stripped bare of all responsibilities, all status and all piety, and free. This is the moment when they nod again to each other, not in greeting, not out of jealousy, but to acknowledge that – flesh and feather, beak and bone – they can be equals in their foolishness.

Their faces now are being shielded by the dusk. What little light there is, is clinging to the surface of the pond. It is so intimate and glistening in that sinking of the day, it's easy for them to exchange the kind of whispered conversation men might have if they shared quarters in a darkened room. It is Jamin who first mentions Tabi's name. He wants to know if there is any word from her. How could there be? the orchardman replies. She did not share her plans with me and does not have a becking angel to bring messages. One moment she was at my side when we were eating, sleeping and at work. And then she'd gone, without a word.

The evening listens to them drying off, to Ebon pulling on his sopping clothes, to Jamin shaking the pond out of his breast and wings. There's silence. Along with the wheezing of cooling trees and the plop of carp taking flies and midges, there is harmony. They are both thinking of the woman, where she might be, what they should do for her as friends.

I miss her, Jamin says, at last. He's blurted it out, as one admitting to a sin, although there is a greater sin he ought to speak of, the sin of being vengeful and consumed by spite — and all for her. But he has begun to hope that, maybe, it's not a failing he'll need to share with anyone. There's just a possibility, he thinks, that his smashing of the barrow and the trug has not been discovered yet or even that it might be brushed aside as something too hurtful and demeaning to be shared. Where is the outraged Alum, after all? I miss your orchard-friend, he repeats, though he is not brave enough to say her name out loud again. What can we do for her? Ebon tilts his head, surprised. We, he starts . . . but has to pause to purse his lips, a nervous smile. He might have overstepped the mark by saying We himself. He would not want to have his nose pecked off. We have to pray for her, he says, believing it to be the answer any angel would expect. We have to ask the lord for forgiveness and beg your brethren to allow her to return. If she is ever found.

Now it's Jamin's turn to tilt his head. He makes a

tetching sound. Prayer is fine and fitting, as far as it goes, he means to imply. But don't forget the liturgy: deeds are a form of prayer, if only lowly ones. Besides, a prayer goes straight into the lord's ear. Then if he speaks of it amongst the priestly angels, they might involve their go-between. Again, the fear he has dismissed just a moment ago comes back to mind. It's Alum wading in, his shard of splintered timber in his hand. It's Alum pelting him with coloured stones. It's a barrow's dreadful squeak. Instead of praying, he suggests, but stops. There is no need to air a blasphemy if it's already carried on the breeze. A spoken word cannot be caught once it's let out. He can almost hear Ebon nodding that he understands what they should do, without its being said. A deed and not a prayer. This has to be unspoken of, Jamin says at last, and kept between the two of us, and witnessed only by the water and my fish, as both are hard of hearing. Alum cannot learn of it. We have to find her, bring her back. If she will come. If she is missing us as well. I have a feeling in my bones . . . His fear and feeling is that eden will remain a diminished and less happy place, unravelling and fraying, until Tabi has returned. I'd fly for her myself, he adds, but – he spreads a wounded wing – I can't go far. Not yet. But you . . .

Ebon nods again. Yesterday he might have shaken his head, scared even to contemplate a visit to the outside world. But this afternoon he's witnessed it himself. He's lobbed an apple into it. He's smelt it and he's tasted it.

133

He's given alms to the gaunt and bony people there, and seen the distance, endless as the sky and time. He's very nearly touched their deadly ground. He's very nearly touched the sacred wall. And he's more plucky now. How can a creature without wings escape from here? he asks.

The stock-pond angel and the orchardman together hatch a plan. At the next full moon, a few days in the waxing yet, Ebon will slip out of his bed around midnight, quite openly, as anybody might if nature calls and, seeming to head off towards the privies, instead proceed . . . creep . . . along the narrower and quieter paths down to the barbican. At that time of the night, the chances of being noticed are not great but, nevertheless, he'll need to be as silent as an owl on wing. The angels will be on their roosts but never quite unconscious and certainly not deaf. Their go-between should be asleep and remarking on his dreams with his usual snores and mutters. Only the almoner might be disturbed and, coming out of the gatehouse where his duties require him both to sleep and to be alert, might spot Ebon waiting, as arranged, hidden from the moonlight by the shadows of a tower, in the tuck where it abuts the garden walls. Or he might be woken by the angel Jamin, a clumsy creature nowadays, who is bound to be more noisy than an owl when he arrives, clutching a rope between his talons and his beak.

But probably, if they are careful and the moon is kind to them, their efforts will be as well-oiled in practice as they are in the planning. Ebon will prepare the rope. All Jamin will need to do is to use his damaged wing to flap his way up to the summit of the wall, hoping that the lord himself is fast asleep and so never learns about these unholy trespasses. Surely he can manage that. It isn't far to fly, but it is too high and smooth to scramble up, even for a practised clamberer like Ebon. He'll loop the rope around a cop stone and let the length fall back onto the ground. Now Ebon will have only to climb, pull up the rope behind him, then drop it on the other side for his descent. Jamin will fly again to retrieve the rope and remove all evidence. Then Ebon can be striding out into the world, his shadow cast ahead of him by the moon and, at dawn, cast behind him by the sun. He'll have the whole day long to find his orchard-friend before return-ing with her, after dark, to the barbican, where Jamin will have returned and rehung the rope for their home-coming. There will be punishments, for sure, but nothing lasts for ever in their everlasting realm. The day will come when they are working side by side again. That's what the plotters make themselves believe.

You need not touch the mortal ground at all, then you'll be safe, Jamin says, though he cannot be sure that there is any truth in that. Ebon chooses to believe that men, like windfalls, become sinners, scamps and scoun-drels, condemned to death, only if soil meets skin. So he plans to be clothed from head to foot and wearing a sun cap and the gloves he uses when there are nettles, thistles or brambles to clear. He will pull on his winter boots. And he will count himself untouchable and safe, so long as he protects his flesh from contact with the world. Except he will not cover up his face. Tabi must see and recognize his face.

She can't be far, he thinks. The world cannot be so very big, so hard to penetrate and search, no matter what the higher angels claim and all the stories that they tell about great skies, wide seas, high peaks, and deserts both of ice and sand. He can't imagine that the lord would allow the earth to be a greater place than eden is. No, Tabi will be spotted straight away, he's sure. The sister and the brother will embrace. They'll have only to wait for night until it's dark enough to climb the rope again. They'll be sleeping side by side, with any luck, by midnight. A blissful rest before discovery. And retribution. It's unlikely but not impossible that then he can pretend – and be believed – that he has never strayed outside at all but spent the day out of sight twined in a tree, perhaps. It's even possible that Tabi's reappearance after so many days might pass or be allowed to pass as evidence that she too hasn't erred like Eve but only hidden herself away for fear of . . . what? For fear of Alum, probably. Nobody would be surprised if Tabi were to play a trick like that or be sorry if Alum were to take the blame. Ebon brightens at the thought. If only Tabi can be found and saved, her reckless escapade and his might not be punished by the lord. He'll have to learn to lie convincingly. She will be proud of me, he thinks, for reuniting her and then for defending her. You love them more than anything, she says, about his care for trees. And anyone? Well, now she'll have his answer, clear as day.

10

EBON IS SUNK in the body hollows of his mattress and dreaming that he's in his orchard raking up the debris and the strew with Tabi at his side, like any normal day, when his sleep is ended by a string of wether bells, no larger than acorns, shaken in his ear. Two kitchen-men, often chosen as Alum's reluctant conscripts when it's demanded – they're in his debt for as yet unreported felonies, so they hardly have a choice – are standing at the dark end of his bed with a coil of toughened twine and a hardwood drinking mazer, slopping with cold water. There are no greetings, just the sort of hurried dedication you might expect from any worker doing any job of which he is ashamed.

Ebon means to offer them his good mornings, as he should, despite their silence and their late attempts to hide their faces in the shadows. But, as he lifts his head from the pillow, a sudden wriggling weight pins him to the bed. It's Alum sitting on his chest, smiling viciously.

Stay very still, he tells the orchardman, and beckons one of his helpers to lean forward and grip his captive by the ankles.

Alum has his open palm pressed down on Ebon's mouth. He wags the pointing finger of his other hand in warning. You're not to make a sound, it says. Or try to struggle free. His neighbours must not wake to witness any scuffle. If any are aroused already by the tinny jangle of the bells, they will turn away and close their eyes, if they are wise.

Ebon can't imagine why he should be gripped and pinioned like a truss of hay by these three men. Perhaps he was observed offending with that windfall and betrayed. Perhaps the gatekeeper himself has decided to report the sacred altar orbs of fruit that concealed the mush in Ebon's basket of alms. Infringements, yes, though only puny ones, deserving a reprimand, no doubt, or exclusion from some evening meals, but nothing more. What else was there that might explain this body squatting on his chest and those shame-faces at his feet?

Ebon has seen other habitants restrained. Tempers can be frayed after a punishing day of work when, say, the earth is heavy or the seasons are unkind or tasks take longer than they should. What once was only irritating amongst his neighbours becomes offensive, given time. It is unseemly but not entirely rare that a man or woman might want to push another or even wrestle them. Then it is a kindness, actually, to pin those angry bodies to the

139

ground, to still those flailing arms and legs, until their hearts and tongues are calmed.

Ebon, though, has never been a man to argue or to push, and so his treatment this morning makes no sense to him. Except that Alum is involved. The man now sitting on his chest has always been too fond of beating compliance into people and disobedience out of them, sometimes with reason though mostly without any. There's hardly a person sleeping in the dormitory who has not been blued and yellowed by his fists. Only yesterday, one of the field-men received two kicks across the backs of his legs and then a slap across his forehead for no greater reason than neglecting to relatch a gate.

Alum takes his knife and shows its gleaming blade to Ebon. Be quiet and still, it is telling him again. He cannot mean to use it on his victim's throat or draw even a bulb of blood. That is the stuff of nightmares or, anyway, the stuff of what goes on outside the wall, where, as everybody has been told a thousand times, the spilling of blood is so commonplace – in wars, in fights, in hunting, in cooking even – that it has lost its holy sacrament and meaning. There within the garden, the sight of blood – hot blood, that is – is rare and horrifying and only might occur by accident. Somebody pulls a hangnail off their finger, possibly, and tears the flesh. A kitchen-worker is too careless with his blade. An orchard-woman snags her shoulder on a branch; the scratch sweats red. A berry-picker gets entangled by the thorns. But blood is rarely drawn in anger or in heat amongst the habitants and never coldly, as a punishment. Such a transgression cannot be allowed on the lord's estate, even by a go-between. Angels can draw human blood, of course, though only with the slightest peck, a warning or a badge of shame.

So Alum's flashing of his knife must be merely mischievous, a little play – and most likely a reminder to Ebon that blades are something he will need to dodge and fear if he ever were to think of stepping into the world as Tabi has. Nevertheless, the threat is still a chilling one. Some accidents are purposeful. The blade is being handled far too recklessly. It's passing close to Ebon's face. He can imagine that a sudden tremble or an only half-intended jerk might nick the soft hem of his nose or slash a lip. Then he'd be breakfasting on blood.

I have permission from the masters, Alum says. I went last evening to their loft. I listed your wrongdoings and I showed the evidence. How you have helped a sister to escape this garden. How you have plans to follow her. How you and she have dined on windfalls, stolen fruit. How you have thrown alms across the garden wall, offending charity. How you, in malice, have smashed and broken our possessions – a barrow and a trug. That alone will cost you dearly. How you have stolen these rare gems to take with you into the world, though no gems in the world will save you from mortality. He reaches under Ebon's pillow and retrieves a purse of coloured stones. You see? Do not deny that I have found them there, secreted in the cushions of your bed. You can't escape the sharpness of my eyes. The greater angels say that I should punish you. Stay still.

Ebon lets the two men lift his legs. He does not even think of kicking them away. He knows they're only doing what they must. If he resists, there'll be four men, and then there will be six. He watches Alum cut the twine to size and split the string of wether bells into two equal lengths. The knife is blunter than it looks, and Alum has to saw against the sinew of the fibre. He shifts his weight and turns his back on Ebon now, still riding him like an animal, and leans forward towards the orchardman's trapped feet. A string of wether bells is wrapped around each of Ebon's ankles and then secured with twine. A longer length of doubled twine is twisted into stronger rope and then tied as a hobble round his shins.

At last, Alum shifts his weight from Ebon's chest and, standing with his two accomplices at the foot of the bed, reaches for the drinking mazer. He tips the water over the three lengths of twine to shrink and tighten every knot. His hand is trembling with the delayed anger of his losses, the trug, the barrow and the orchard-woman. He wishes that the water was hot oil. The waste runs down onto the blankets and the mattress underneath. Ebon will have to sleep in a wet bed tonight, as well as spend the day in pond-drenched clothes, still damp from his encounter with Jamin.

Again, Alum wags a warning finger. This time it says, Don't touch. This is the lord's twine. Don't think of cutting it or snapping it. Disobey and we might have to swap the strings for chains. There are iron anklets in the store. They'll suit you very well. The angels are concerned for you, he says at last, his voice controlled and threatening. Their little bells are meant only to keep you close to them. And me. You will be walking music for our ears. We'll always know your whereabouts. If only she – he does not want to voice her name – had been shackled with a string of bells, like you are now, we'd not have lost her to . . . He lifts his hand. To goodness knows what, his fingers say. And you'd not have brought this on yourself. Now you have only your own weakness to blame, for thinking of abandoning the lord. So, stand and walk. Your day begins. The three men step away and go as quietly as they can outside, taking the mazer, the knife and the little purse of coloured stones with them. The dormitory door bangs noisily. As if by sorcery, the usual waking bell sounds at exactly that moment. Ebon's neighbours start to stir and sit up in their beds. They stretch their arms and muss their hair and flex their legs. The unfed night has left them stiff and listless. It is another working day.

Ebon has not spoken yet this morning. He's not even muttered underneath his breath. He is too baffled and too shocked, both by the truth he's heard on Alum's lips – the forbidden windfall he pulled open with his teeth only yesterday, the alms apple that he clodded over the battlement for all to see – and by the untruths too. He'd never seen those stones before or, indeed, their fancy purse. He wouldn't dare or even want to damage anybody's tools or implements, especially those that have been fashioned with such effort and such love. He played no part at all in Tabi's flight and would have stopped her if he could. It's true, he does have freshly minted plans to follow her, but he has not shared them with anyone except . . . except a chilling thought: the only way the go-between can know of them for sure is if Jamin, the all too friendly and persuasive angel at the pond, has netted him and landed him and dished him up as he might an eel. How else can this have come about?

The suspicion that he has been duped and then betrayed by an angel is so winding and dumbfounding that Ebon can hardly catch his breath. He certainly cannot find the heart to speak when one or two of his neighbours wish him well for the day as they head out for work. He just sits alone on the edge of his bed until the dormitory has emptied with his hands on his knees, looking down on the bells, the hobble and the knots. Fair punishment, in many ways, for being such an innocent. He has been lured and duped by one word, We.

His walk down to the orchard is a tinkling but a sombre one. The twine shackles are not heavy or too tight, at least not for a man as hard-skinned and muscular

144

as Ebon, and the hobble between his legs is long enough to allow an almost hearty stride, though it sags and catches on the rims of uneven paving stones. But these are intended not to restrain him but to shame him and to parade his shame to anyone he meets. Every step he takes is a jangling reminder of his indignity. Anklets made of iron and connected with a chain would be no greater punishment, he thinks, and might be less noisy and less mocking. Even when he stands quite still, his flimsy anklets seem to chatter on. Half-wit, tinkle-wit, dimwit, dolt, they say. Ninny, nitwit, numbskull, clod. Last night he fell asleep approving of himself and of the plan he'd hatched with Jamin for finding Tabi in the world and bringing her back home. Now he only counts himself to be an angel's fool. Their plan was a fantasy, never intended to be carried out, and dreamed up only as a trap. Instead, once the full moon has started to wane, Ebon won't be sleeping side by side with Tabi but sharing his damp bed with anklets, tethers, twine and bells. It seems clear to him that the cunning of the masters was greater than he ever thought. Those two – the go-between together with that seeming kindly angel at the pond – were not the enemies they feigned to be but sly confederates. Together they had dipped their nets and lured him in. He is now as helpless as a fish, drowning in the very air it breathes. Well, that's to be expected, he supposes. Angels only look out for themselves.

*

EBON'S TASK TODAY, as is usual once a fast is over, is to pick unblemished fruit for that night's second course. There are good pears high in the trees which are bound to have scarred skins, such is the disobliging nature of a pear. But, peeled and sliced, they will be sweet and tasty in a pie. He's known mostly as the trusted orchardman, but pudding king is his second name and the one used most affectionately. If he is more valued and respected than many of his fellows, it's not only that the frequent priestly homilies about Adam, Eve and the sacredness of fruit enhance his standing in their eyes but also – more so, in fact – because of what his care and labour bring to the supper table, the treats that can be relished for their sweetness rather than just endured – as grains and turnips are – for their stodgy nourishment. Even in the fastnesses of winter, the cooks can go down to their cellars and return with dried plums and gages or shrunken bullaces or cherries jarred in juice, as well as pears and apples that the pudding king has wrapped and stored for them. They'll make bygone pies, as they are called, which taste, if anything, even sweeter than the younger, summer ones. Then, when they are served, there's not a habitant who doesn't nod with gratitude to both Ebon and his Tabi for all their harvesting. Only the sister who maintains the hives and provides the honey can count herself more popular.

So even on the worst of days – and this is one – Ebon relishes the picking. He takes stock, seeing where his efforts will be best rewarded. The ground is strewn below the trees with mushy fallen fruit. One or two of the fruits are firm and not too badly bruised, but Ebon is not tempted today to flout the law and add them to his basket. He's come to realize that everything he does or says is known and noted by his enemies. Instead, he kicks them fiercely off into the grass, one for Alum and a second for Jamin. He's split and damaged them, but the kicks are not as hard and satisfying as he might have hoped. His hobble and the twine get in the way. The strings of bells clang out in mockery with every move. It would be easy to silence them, he knows. One blow from his garden axe and the twine would split in two. But he is wary of that twine, and wisely so. It is the angels' chosen leash and, if he severs it, he will have severed links with them as well. It is an article of faith which he should no more hack away than his own arm.

It's better not to dwell on his misfortunes, he decides, but rather to find escape in work. Against good sense, he'll scale the trees – an easy task in normal times – and pluck the few remaining pears that are still hanging from their stalks. Climbing is, of course, more difficult and perilous when he is hobbled. It's not that he's especially restricted in the stretch or reach of his legs, it's mostly that the twine snags on the jut of branches, or lodges round the spurs and collars of the bark, or gets caught amongst the twigs. Then he has to descend a risky step or two to unsnag himself and try again, until the next time he is hooked or caught. Climbing trees – his calling and his joy – has never been so treacherous. He knows that Tabi's just as much to blame for this as are Alum and Jamin. She has been thoughtless, he concedes. And self-ish, possibly. Yet he, so far, is the only one to have to pay a price for it. He cannot, though, stop missing her.

Ebon has collected a basketful of pears quite quickly, despite the shackles. The favoured tree is almost bare. There is a single plump fruit, nicely reddened in the sun, almost out of reach but irresistible. It cannot just be left for birds. So Ebon ventures higher than he's been before on this tree and has to risk all his weight on a clearly brittle branch that groans and promises to snap. With his arm extended to its limits and his feet spread wide, he has the last pear at his fingertips. He tugs it free, and staggers back on its release. Should he fall, he'll end up looking even sillier. He'll be swinging upside down, hanging from his twine with no way to escape except to call for help or summon it with little bells. You look just like an unplucked fruit yourself, whoever comes is bound to say when they find him pending like a pear. Let's make a pie from you. Let's peel you, pip you, worm you, slice you. No, the name he'll call out as he swings, and as the blood is rushing to his skull, is obviously the woman's. From where he is, he can just make out the growing stabs and scratches in the bark that represent her face. He knows she cannot come to help, not in the flesh. She's not in earshot any more. But naming her out loud – as he does now – is all that there remains of her. He can imagine an eternity with nothing left but names.

He is still struggling with the climb – the clambering down, which proves even more difficult than the ascent – when Alum arrives, more silently than usual. He has no barrow and no squeak. Their loss is scorned by Ebon's chit-chat bells. The angels' man just stands a little distance off, his hands on his hips, and watches. He doesn't bother with a greeting. He hasn't come to be polite or brotherly. He doesn't want to justify himself or even hurt the man again. There is time enough for that. He simply wants to make his presence felt and let the orchardman understand that the punishment for smashing tools – for being liked by everyone, as well – must be a long and bitter one. Nevertheless, he is in time to hear the fellow mutter to himself, as he attempts to shin down from his tree. This is not the first time of late that he has overheard Ebon calling out Tabi's name. For a moment, Alum even thinks that she must be close enough to hear, that she has been hiding in the orchard all this time or that she has returned, and Ebon is addressing her. He cannot help but swing around and check the treetops behind him for a shape or shadow in their crowns. He's seen her there so many times before, at ease, at home, the brightest blossom and the sweetest fruit, amongst the branches of the trees.

But, no, the hobbled pudding king is merely talking to himself. The spoken name expresses sorrow and desire.

That smiley man's not smiling any more. Yet Alum cannot squeeze much pleasure out of that. He understands the aching hollowness of sorrow and desire. In the deepest moments of his night, when he's most troubled by himself and by the chilling silence of the day to come, he has been known to name the friends he has not got, the company that he will never keep, the sisters and the brothers who shy away from him. He intends only to yell out Ebon's name so that the man high in his tree can be in no doubt that the angels' eyes are watching him, and that the angels' ears are hearing him, or at least can trace his bells, and that the angels' nose, their go-between, is smelling him.

Ebon, Alum calls, as sternly as he can. Ebon turns towards his name and once again today is mystified. He hasn't heard a warning but a plea. The two men catch each other's eyes and for a moment look across the orchard at each other, unified in ways beyond their expectations.

11

IT IS FULL moon, the last one of the season. By the time it has waned and slivered, most of the pickings in the garden will have been gathered in. The kitchen-hands have done their best to put together a farewell summer meal for the evening with the last few squashes, some watery tomatoes puckered with age, mint leaves, flat beans and peppers, all past their prime, perhaps, but freshly torn from the stem and tasty in a stew, with salt. They'll finish with the pears the pudding king has picked. Tomorrow and the months ahead can only offer winter food from the pickle jars, the dry storage baskets, and the clamps of compacted straw where turnips and potatoes are taking refuge from the cold.

This final bulging harvest moon marks both the end of plenty and the shortening of days. Rarely does the darkness seem so generous. Backs and shoulders tested by the summer months of labour can stay a good deal longer in their beds and then get up to, sometimes, nothing more testing than some tidying or pruning. The spade and scythe give way to brooms and brushes. The working days of winter are more communal. Everybody forages dead wood for the log stacks or gathers with rakes to bag up fallen leaves for mulch. Together they will plough and trench the resting fields, sharing both the weight of the earth but also the hefty tiredness when they fall exhausted into bed. Then, on those rare afternoons when they are met with snow or mighty winds or heavy mire, they are allowed to stay indoors for weaving, potting, carpentry and mending. And talk. Not everyone is sad to see the back of summer, not least because this year it's ending on a fretful note. Winter, surely, will be less tense. So the farewell meal is festive and enjoyable rather than regretful. Even Ebon – now his ankles are concealed beneath a table and his bells, if he stays still, are mostly silent – is at ease, forgetting for the moment what the full moon might have meant for him. And for Tabi.

At midnight, though, Jamin is waiting in the courtyard at the barbican. Exactly as arranged. He has a length of sturdy rope which he has borrowed from the belfry tower. He's kept his distance from the guardhouse, where the keeper, recently returned from his last summer meal with his fellows, is already fast asleep. Jamin can hear his snuffles and his snores and further off, amongst the trees and undergrowth, the bustle and the stir of animals. Beyond the wall, the ghosts are calling as they often do at this time of the night. There's laughter that is inexplicable, and hollow cries. And dogs.

Jamin does not think he has been spotted yet by anyone that matters. When he came out into the night, he made sure his angel brethren were not disturbed on their roosts and then checked that the doors to the lofts where the priestly angels passed their time were firmly closed. Luckily, he saw Alum sloping off to bed. That is a man who is evidently so free of doubt he sleeps as soundly as a log and doesn't wake till light. So Jamin feels that all is well. Their plan's in place. They will not be discovered. Although the moon is full, the cloud is thick and low. Occasionally there is a finger of light breaking through the gloom and shadowing the courtyard for a moment, but tonight the moon might just as well be new for all the lucy it provides.

Jamin stretches out both wings. The damaged one is shorter than the good but, since he spoke with Ebon, he has spent the days flexing it in readiness for their venture. He senses that some of its power has returned since his tumble. He's even tried a few short flights across the pond and, though they were not gainly, he was at least airborne for long enough to revive his self-confidence and recognize that, possibly, his injury was not as limiting as he has chosen to believe. Reaching the summit of the barbican wall and coiling a rope should not be difficult. Nor should coming back down into the courtyard, though in his practice flights his landings were not elegant or soft.

Tonight he is a little nervous, nevertheless. His crop and gullet are at war. He has thought of nothing else for days. This escapade. This disobedience. This . . . he hardly dares to think the word . . . this blasphemy. He's not sure what it should be called or how it will be judged and punished if his part in it is revealed. His nightmares have been troubling, but when awake his hopes are greater than his fears. It's not impossible that Ebon's trip into the world could be a fruitful one. After all, the orchardman has all day to find their Tabi. Reason says that she will not have ventured far but will be lurking near the outer wall, comforted perhaps by any sounds that might escape from eden while she either adapts to coping on her own or comes to realize she cannot. How will she feed herself, without a garden to provide her meals? How will she stay safe without the lord's eye watching her? Where will she rest her head at night, without a pillow to her name, and without a name to her face? She's bound to want to come back home . . . if she's alive, that is. For who's to say or know what might occur when habitants of the lord's garden stray beyond its hems? There is no reason to believe that death will take its time, not baring its sharp fangs until, say, another hundred seasons pass. It could be that anyone who follows Eve and Adam there will perish with the first breath they draw. A gasp of it, and then the orchard-girl is lost. The orchardman who follows her will perish too, the moment that he lets go of the angel's rope and spreads his feet across the solid ground. They'll be moon folk, the pair of them, waning to a sliver in the memories of all the wiser souls who stay put in eden. If they live on at all, it will be only in sermons, as warnings in the stories the greater angels tell.

But if they both come back, and in good shape? Then nothing's lost, he dares to hope against all reason. Then all is well. Then eden can relax again. Then winter will be whole and calm. And he, Jamin, might be regarded as a saviour of the lord's estate.

An owl is calling and Jamin pricks up his ears. It might not be a bird at all but a hoot from Ebon, to say he's getting close. He's overdue already. The night is wearing on. But then the owl repeats its call and Jamin can see its smug outline perching in the canopy, waiting for the chance to kill. It's baffling and unnerving to be waiting there alone. Ebon is normally the sort to be on time, especially for a rendezvous such as tonight's, when he must have hoped to be united with his great friend. There has to be a reason for his lateness. Maybe Alum has been up to further mischief.

Jamin rehearses prayers and hymns to still his nerves and pass the time, but, even though the moon has now emerged above the canopy and edged into an empty quarter of the sky, there isn't any sign of Ebon. The midnight darkness has already thinned, as has the angel's confidence. Finally, he decides to leave the rope in the corner of the courtyard for the time being and test his wings again to see if he can discover what's delayed the man. He has seen Ebon only once since they devised their plan and just in passing, from afar. The orchardman was not his usual open self but evasive, hostile even. He did not square up in greeting but narrowed himself, turning sideways on, as if to make himself less visible and beyond hearing. Jamin tried and failed to catch his eye. It was perplexing and disheartening. That is why the angel's in a flap and he's hurrying – in semi-flight, like a chicken, and with a pounding heart – along the spokes back to the buildings at the garden's hub.

The open ground around the dormitory and angel lofts is even darker than the courtyard at the barbican. What little moonlight makes it through the clouds is trapped in the branches of the windbreak firs. Their silhouette is swaying slightly in the breeze. It's eerie there when there are no habitants or angels going about their chores. Every sound is sinister. Jamin half hopes he'll find the orchardman sitting outside in the dark, having lost his nerve for this adventure and wanting only just a little nudge of encouragement, some reassurances. So, first of all, he circles all the buildings, even daring once or twice to call out. Ebon, show yourself. But in the end he has to do what he dreads most, and that is to creep into the great long dormitory where Ebon might be either sleeping or awake but failing to find courage.

Jamin's qualms about entering the dormitory are not entirely merited. An angel is allowed to check on garden-hands. Even in the middle of the night. Even if the angel is Jamin, the lowest of the high. He shakes his feathers, sheds his fears and pulls the rope to lift the latch on the door. He is in luck. The workings have been recently oiled and so the door swings back with hardly a sound. It's pitch dark in there, but angels' eyes are sharp. He can make out the shapes of bodies and of beds and hear the wheezes and the creaks of sleep, so different from the sound of angels in their lofts, their feathers ruffling, their billing and their cooing.

Jamin has never truly liked the smell of habitants, especially those who toil out in the fields and stink of weariness and earth. Even Tabi when she's close reminds him of the scent of mushrooms. For all her sweetness in his pond-side bower, she is damp on the breath. But he is shocked to discover how ripe the dormitory is at night. The snuffles and the belching stale the air, especially on a chilly full moon like this, when the wooden casements are kept closed against both the cold and the chance of penetrating light. He feels as if he's breathing smoke. Compared to this, his pond is fragrant.

He edges along the length of the narrow walkway at the foot of the beds, looking for a shapeless one or, at least, one not offering a living sound or smell. He pauses when his feet land on creaking boards and stays quite still until he's certain that no one there has woken up. His main concern is not to rouse the occupant of the furthest bed, the one set slightly apart from all the others at the far end of the dormitory, for that's where Alum will be found, by all reports. He passes forty beds, including the two bare-timbered frames where Eve and Adam rested once, before he finds what he believes to be a newly empty one. He presses his beak against the coverlets, just to check there is no body there. The bedding's odourless, apart from the sallow smell of cloth. If she's slept there, all traces of her have entirely disappeared. His beak and face are still pressed into the cloth when, at his back, he is aware of someone sitting up in bed, looking round. It will be Alum, he is sure. The man knows everything and misses nothing, even in his sleep.

But then Jamin hears the very faintest tinkling of bells as the body in the forty-second bed turns over in its blanketing. A hand comes out, as it has done a hundred times before and stretches through the muffled darkness of the aisle between his place and hers to check the covers are no longer shaped by Tabi. But, unlike those other disappointing nights, this time the beating hollow of Ebon's heart is not greeted by the silent hollow of her mattress or the solemn hush of all those dreaming solitudes in all the other beds. Instead his fingers land on warm and breathing feathers. He knows at once what they must be. But whose, he cannot tell.

It's just as well that Ebon was startled in his sleep and then briefly shielded by the building's darkness from knowing for sure whose feathers he has touched. If he was fully awake and not dreaming of much happier days and if it were light, he'd not allow Jamin any chance of talking or explaining. He sits up fully in his bed, however, and seems to know at once that there is urgency and danger. He does not make a sound. I waited for you, Jamin says. The moon is full. We were agreed . . . They cannot see each other's features yet but voices on their own are eloquent. What Ebon hears is someone telling him the truth. And then — as the angel's face becomes discernible — he sees it being spoken, for Jamin's eyes have widened rather than narrowed, as they might have done if he were telling lies. And his mouth stays open when he isn't speaking. It is not pursed. Deceiving angels must surely purse their beaks — as men and women purse their lips — to stop the truth escaping, whereas a master who is open-mouthed has nothing to conceal.

So Ebon lets the angel have his say at the bedside, and then, when they hear the unmistakable snuffling of Alum in the stub end of the room, they creep outside into the open ground and huddle below the firs, where they are less likely to be heard. Or caught. To get there, Ebon, with one of his blankets wrapped around his shoulders and kept from slipping by the grip of his chin, has to shuffle down the walkway in his sleeping clothes, holding his twine shackle in one hand and his boots in the other, and doing his best to proceed with just the slightest tinkling of bells. The man has seldom been so cumbersome or slow.

Outside, the soughing of the wind amongst the trees, the night-time itchings in the undergrowth, drown out the conversation of the two conspirators as they walk in almost moonlit harmony down to the barbican, whispering promises, offering apologies, providing awkward explanations and, at last, brokering a truce. I beg forgiveness, Jamin says. The angel begs forgiveness from the man!

It takes Jamin fewer than a dozen pecks to break Ebon's twine in half. Detaching the anklets and the bells is more difficult. The knots were soaked in water by Alum and his men, and even Ebon's tough and practised fingernails cannot loosen them. Jamin has to slide his beak between his companion's ankles and the twine and pull and twist and saw until it snaps. He's careful not to make a further noise when he carries the bells and the pieces of twine off the path and hides them in the undergrowth. He looks around for landmarks, to help remember their hiding place. Those bells will have to be reclaimed and then retied.

Ebon's shins and ankles are grazed and tender, though there is hardly any blood. They will be dark with bruises by dawn. No matter, Ebon says. Bruises count for little on a night when he might very well, once time has done its work, end up just like that jack has ended up, as light and limbless as a stain or smell. If only he were in bed, asleep and calm, instead of being toppled out of it into the perils of the night. He's been a fool to think he could be bold. But, now that the twine and bells have been removed, he is revitalized. It feels as if he has been released from the weightiest of shackles. He tries some playful twirls, some kicks, a little skipping dance, to pump energy into his veins. And it is at that moment, with the barbican now a silhouette in sight, that both of them accept that their plans — their hurried and fool-hardy plans — will go ahead because their love for Tabi says there is no better choice. If not tonight, then when? If not tonight, then never.

The sky is cloudy still but there is light behind them, not from the moon but from the east. They can't delay, for dawn is seeping in already. When Jamin left the courtyard earlier, the barbican was almost shapeless. The night, the shadow and the masonry were one. The only colour was the rare and distant yellow of a star. But now the greys and blacks are turning green and brown, though any yellow in the stars is muted by the waxing light.

They do not dare to speak. The gatekeeper must be stirring now. It is his duty to be dressed and up before the sun. Ebon retrieves the coil of rope from its hiding place in the corner of the courtyard and lifts it up while Jamin decides which end to hold it by, and whether he should use his talons or his beak. And then he flexes, stretches out his wings. The keeper, hearing it, might take it for a gust of wind. There is an awkward jump, a little treading of the air, a moment when the weight negotiates for buoyancy, a twinge of pain along the wounded bone, a flap, a thrust, and then some sudden elegance, a stormy rush of air, that's all, a dappled promise of a greater blue, and he's aloft. The coil of rope comes suddenly to life, twisting and rising, as the angel flaps above.

In scarcely a moment, Jamin lands on the flat pavings between the outer and the inner battlements but does not dare to pause to look around or to settle his beating heart. His flight was only short but he is exhausted, as much by the tension as by the effort he has made with his neglected wing. He loops the rope around a solid cop, looks down to check that Ebon has secured the other end with his foot, and then – with more elegance than during his ascent – flies down to earth again with his end of the rope. He has to draw his breath before he speaks. Tomorrow, then, he says. At midnight. Please trust in me. I will have put the rope back in place – I promise it – but hanging down the other side. For you. For both of you. Go now.

Ebon's used to climbing. Now's not the time to wonder what awaits. He ties his blanket round his throat like a cloak and spits on his palms, for the better grip and to protect his skin against the rough fibres. He takes the loose ends of the rope and twists them tightly into a single sinew. He finds his angle, puts his feet onto the stone, braces his legs . . . and walks, using the mortar troughs in the masonry as shallow toeholds and paying out the rope behind him as he does so. Loose stones and debris tumble to the ground but not for long enough, they hope, to disturb the keeper's sleep. Ebon really ought to take more care with where he puts his feet. He hardly pauses at the top – if it's a trespass and a blasphemy, keep it short – but quickly pulls the rope after him, untwists it and reverses it so that both ends now hang freely down into the world.

Then he descends. He is surprised to discover that the wall has a deep, jutting overhang along the whole length of the mortal side; the lord has made it nigh impossible for anyone to climb up and over from there. But once he has swung and dangled for a moment, his feet are dragging on the ground in the damp hollows of the moat and he can stand. He stays a moment in the lee of the wall, waiting to hear the labour of the angel's second flight, his landing on the summit to retrieve the rope. Then Ebon's on his way. He does not turn to watch the rope being unlooped from its cop and taken off by Jamin. He trusts his angel once again, entirely. All Ebon has to do for now is to find a place where he can safely – and warmly – spend what little's left of night.

163

12

ALUM IS NOT sleeping well. The evening's final fruits sit heavy in his stomach. He has pains across his chest which he can ease with belching. He does so noisily. Better out than in. Then for a while he manages to nap before the wind builds up and he must belch again. So he is only half asleep when he hears the latch being lifted on the dormitory door.

It is not unusual to hear the latch at this time of the night. Nature makes haphazard calls on the many bladders sleeping there. The door is always kept well-oiled so that the comings and the goings to the latrines do not disturb the sleepers. Sometimes the going and the coming back are far too swift, then Alum knows one of the habitants has only stepped outside and released his waters – it's usually a man – onto the open ground beyond the door. That's not allowed. If Alum can identify the culprit from his shape as he comes back or by the number of steps he takes to reach his bed, he can impose some punishments the next day: collecting kack from the latrines for boostering manure and bucketing piss for making bleach and dye are the most fitting and the most detested. His victims are astounded when they're caught. Alum knows about their every spit and pee, even when he's sleeping and his back is turned. The man has eyeballs in his arse.

So when he hears that latch, he listens carefully, hoping to astound another rule breaker. But someone's coming in, not going out, it seems. This person's hesitant and shuffling. It doesn't sound as if bare feet are hastening, as quietly as they can, on wooden boards, but more that something soft and pillowy is wheezing down the walkway at the end of the beds. Alum only has to open half an eye to recognize, against what little light there is, the tucked-in, narrow-shouldered shape of an angel with his wings held close. He thinks first that his services are being called upon, that very soon he'll feel his covers being lifted off by some demanding beak. But then he notices that one of the angel's wings does not sit quite flat against his side but elbows out, a gawky branch. It's that stinking fish, Jamin.

Alum lies as still as he can, hardly breathing, though he has to swallow a belch and digest the pain. He listens to the creaking of the boards and the angel's anxious pausing before a few more hesitant steps. And then there is the faintest tinkling of bells as Ebon is woken. The go-between knows at once that mischief is afoot and what that mischief is. He has always known that the apple and

165

the fish would conspire to reunite that second Adam with his Eve. She is a burr who sticks to any creature that comes close. He knows that, all too well. Even in her absence – more so, possibly – she encumbers even him, the tough-hearted Alum, both as a burden and a care. She is the one who brought Ebon crashing down upon his barrow and his trug. She is the one who, from afar, continues to inhabit him.

He shuts his eyes completely now. There seems to be a whispered argument. Alum cannot make out every word but he catches Tabi and We agreed and rope. He hears Ebon sitting up in bed, then shuffling slowly along the walkway – his strings of ankle bells almost silenced – before going out into the night.

Alum pulls on his boots and clothes as quickly as he can and follows the conspirators. He brings the heavy cudgel which, ever since the spoiling of his trug and barrow, he has adopted as his instrument of rank. The bright blue cloth around its handle is meant to represent the clout of angels. He has to wait behind the dormitory door because he can hear Ebon's and Jamin's voices – first sounding bitter and then more honeyed – in the open ground below the firs. He waits too long. When finally he dares to step outside, his quarries have very nearly disappeared. He can just make out the distant budging of the darkness and the faintest tinkling of bells which less practised ears might mistake for jangle moths or just the rustle of a bush. It doesn't matter, though, if he loses sight of them. He has already decided where they must be heading. To the thickets and the ivy swags and to the tree which yearns its great flat bough into the world beyond. He knows the quickest route and can be there before them. He'll start below the forest's heavy canopy in the lord's own wilderness, and then he'll race along the bouldered ridge, down the path between the garden wall and the pales of sharpened timbers, to reach the great trees in the sunken gully and what, he persuades himself, must be their passage of escape.

It is hard going, especially at night, with the moon bashful and unobliging, behind clouds. The paths are scarcely visible. Alum stumbles several times, on stones and clods and unseen root runs. He cracks his shins. He blunders through nettles and into thorns, snagging his clothes and tearing his skin, and swinging his cudgel blindly in the hope of opening the path. But he is driven forward by the prospect of preventing a great sin. How grateful the priestly angels will be. They will be satisfied with him. He's caught a fallen angel on the wing and a man edging on a flattened bough towards mortality.

No one's at the tree when he arrives, so he has time enough to find a hiding place nearby and to plan what he will do when, he supposes, one of them attempts to fly – or flap – and the other one prepares to climb. That surely is their plan. He has to smile – the very thought of it. He'll grab them by their ankles when they've barely

167

left the ground and then, if they resist, his cudgel can persuade them to obey.

Yet, though he waits for long enough for even the slowest walkers to reach his hiding place, the angel and the orchardman do not appear. The forest is quiet and undisturbed. He is the only creature there, apart from insects, rodents, birds. If he stays still and holds his breath, he can sense nothing other than the hammer of his heart and the salt of weeping. His are despairing, mildewed tears, as unexpected and unsummoned as a bead of sweat. The darkness and the throbbing silence are too much to bear. The days ahead, the seasons and the years, crowd in on him but do not offer any love or joy or even touch, unless it is the touch of seizing sisters by the wrists, the joy of striking brothers with his fists, the love of blunting other people's happiness. A go-between is not embraced. He hugs himself across the chest to squeeze out any further tears and stop himself from trembling. So, behold the man. And so behold the everlasting heart and what it has endured and what it must endure. He lets out a sigh, at last, and as he does so overhears the distant slap of something on the masonry. He holds his breath again and turns towards the sound, which is repeated. This time he can hear some debris falling to the ground and the scrambling of feet or feathers. It's coming from the barbican.

Alum knows at once he has misjudged – he's fooled himself, indeed – where Jamin and Ebon were heading at

168

this unholy hour. They have a simpler, less strenuous plan than what he has expected. A length of rope is help enough to scale the garden wall anywhere. Why bother with those ivy swags or boughs? Why snag yourself on thorns? An angel with an injured wing would want to stay away from these thickets, these gullies and these tripping paths, for fear of damaging another. So they are in the open courtyard, then, making their escape by planting their deceitful claws and hands on the sacred battlement.

The courtyard isn't very far away. He thumbs the teardrops from his eyes, spits out their taste and summons the energy to run. His cudgel, weighty though it is, seems to make the going easier. The path is widening in front of him as if it means to be a help. He hardly makes a sound. His feet are light. He's almost flying, you might say. The hunt might have made him tearful but strong and supple too. He bursts into the open ground of the barbican's courtyard in time to see the last of Ebon – just his head – in silhouette, descending from the summit of the wall into the world. Then he spots the angel, Jamin, stretching out his wings and gathering his strength for flight. It is ungainly to behold, especially in this semi-darkness, when the feathers are not even hinting blue but are just weight and mass and shadow. All that Alum sees is a transgression taking place. He is too aroused and thrilled to take proper stock or pay heed to any cares and cautions. He has his cudgel in his hand and the force of duty at his back, propelling him with its almighty wind. If his allegiance to the priestly angels – and to the greater lord in his high realms – counts for anything at all, this is what he is required to do.

Jamin is in the air, at barely shoulder height, when he hears the thud of running feet and the cries of some protesting man. His first instinct is to think that Ebon has fallen from the rope or is facing danger on the other side. But the mayhem is coming from the courtyard itself. There is a burst of sound and energy, the quickening clomp of boots, the grunt of someone swinging out his arms, a turbulence of air, and then the crash of cudgel hitting flesh with anger and with force. Alum means it to be more punishing than that used on his barrow and his trug. Luckily the first blow, though hard, catches Jamin only on his flank where there is fat but little bone. It's not enough to bring the angel down to earth, though for a moment he is labouring his wings, made bulky in the air. He's hurt and shocked but still he manages to stay aloft and does his best to gain more height. An instinct tells him that he must. Whoever's hitting him will want to test the limits of eternity.

The second blow almost misses Jamin entirely, hitting just the bone and sinew of his hind toe. He has escaped, for the moment. He stands, puffed and chastened, with his damaged toe, on the flat top of the battlement. There is time enough to glimpse the distant outline of Ebon, his blanket flapping as he runs, fleeing from the wall. He is too far away already to have heard the affray at the barbican. Jamin turns towards the courtyard where the dawn is shedding just sufficient light for him to see first the keeper rushing from his room, half dressed and panicking, and then a little further back the unmistakable cocky frame of the angels' go-between, his mouth flecked with spittle and his body bloody from the thorns he's hurtled through. There's a swinging cudgel in his hand. He's taking careful aim. He throws. And he throws well for such a meagre man.

Jamin is struck across his back but the force behind the throw weakens in its upwards flight. The cudgel only glances him, enough to ruffle feathers, not to bruise. It clatters across the overhang, down the far side of the wall and lands between the two coiled rope ends which Jamin will not now have the chance to recover and to hide for the next night's rendezvous. The second missile Alum throws is the night pot full of piss from outside the gatehouse door. Jamin does not intend to feel the weight or splash of that. He knows at once the game is up for him. He is a fallen angel now, a renegade. He has displaced himself from any bower, any loft or any holy realm. He is either friendless, masterless and free, or he is a prisoner.

And so he flies again. Taking off is easier from such a lofty place. He scuttles only half a dozen steps and then he simply has to lift and arch his wings and he is in the air. He is surprised to feel so strong and capable. It is as if he's never damaged himself or, indeed, has not been cudgelled on his flank or toe, or pelted on the wall with anything the go-between can find to throw. His body is aflame with unaccustomed energy. His veins are pumping life and hope as well as dread and fear. For who knows what the dawn might bring? What retributions might there be? Or what rewards? For once, though, it is clear what he must do and what his duty is. He does not need to land or touch the ground. He has only to stay aloft and, like a buzzard, eye the earth below until he finds, as find he must, some trace of Ebon in the world. He'll spread his wings and cast a shadow on the man. And then, when Ebon lifts his head to look, this great blue angel in the sky can tell the orchardman, Beware.

13

THE DARKNESS IS a blanket for a while, still vaguely warm from yesterday, but dawn's first hint of light, before the sun has risen high enough to bare its face, is tormenting and cold. Ebon, longing for his proper bed, has rarely felt so stiff. He has discovered a first certainty about the outside world. It's frostier than eden. He is concealed in a stony hollow beneath a thicket of thorn and bramble where there are blackberries to be eaten for his breakfast, their drupelets glistening with dew. They need cutting back and taming, but they taste almost the same as the tended garden berries, a bit rougher and more peppery, perhaps. He dares to try only a couple, though. He won't be seen if he stays still and does not disturb the brambles, even when the light is up. The screen of stems and branches is too dense. So far, so good, he mutters to himself a dozen times. For there he is, alive and breathing beyond the wall of eden.

Soon, once he is warm enough to dare, he will peer

between the leaves, look out at an emerging day and decide how he might find his lost and lonely friend, and yet be undiscovered. He cannot merely shout her name, although his instincts tell him she is close. He knows he has to stay invisible, unheard. He's fearful, actually, of the world's boundless uncertainties. If it were just another eden – predictable and regular – he could expect simply to see her walking by. It is a rare day in the garden which draws to a close before he's at least glimpsed if not spoken to all his brothers and his sisters. Even if he has missed one or two in the working light, they will be sharing his table for their meals or sleeping close to him at night. Nobody remains unseen or unheard for long before it's noticed. In eden, no concealment or withdrawal remains a private matter. Their flock's too small for that. Their lives are manifest. But here?

Ebon's listened many times to the angels' talk of multitudes beyond their walls but where's the proof? He hasn't yet heard the cough or chatter of a single soul. So far, this seems to be an empty, silent place, unhabited. The score or so of faces he saw retrieving alms at the barbican might be the only ones there are in this undiscovered world. Yet he can't be sure. There's no denying that the distances he's glimpsed are huge, beyond imagining. This is not a garden tightly girdled round but something vast and borderless. A sister could walk ten thousand steps and still not blunt her nose against a battlement.

Ten thousand steps? The thought of them makes Egon reconsider. Knowing Tabi as he does, he cannot doubt she'd want to reach the last of those and then the next step and the next. It's not unlikely that she might have started running and not stopped until she reached those frontiers without frontiers that the angels talk and sermonize about, the lengths and breadths and spaces, world without end, amen.

Let's hope those frontiers are no more than half a day's walk away, he thinks. He has only until midnight. Then Jamin will come to the barbican again to hang the rope in place for his – for their – return. It won't be as easy as he'd hoped. That overhang would be a challenge for anyone, even with a rope, even if they spend their lives climbing high, as he and Tabi do. Perhaps they can make a pulley of some kind or tie knots for footholds. Whatever happens, Ebon must regain the garden before tomorrow's dawn.

For the moment, though, he has to rest on stony ground beneath the brambles and the thorns. It's dry enough but wintry. There is still a penetrating breeze which no thicket in the world could blunt entirely. The bed-time clothes he was wearing when he crept unprepared out of the dormitory are thin and loose. He has a blanket to wrap around his shoulders, but he has chosen instead to spread it on the ground and sit on it, rather than risk the life-ending contact of the soil. Whatever death turns out to be, it's best avoided, isn't it? What is

175

it the angels say? It takes only a moment and a toe, and death will sink its teeth into your foot and death will syphon the blood from your veins, to make room for its phantoms and its ghosts. But then he recalls what Tabi says, whenever she is in one of her impish moods. It's possible, she likes to tell her brothers and her sisters, who all must have thought the same a thousand times but never dared to say so, that life beyond the palisades is paradise. And eden is a lesser place! The sermons teach the labourers inside to think that their estate is measure-less contentment and the outside world is little more than famine, pestilence and suffering. Great is their sorrow and fathomless their pain. But who's to say, unless they find out for themselves? Who's to say, indeed, that there is even death out there unless you are prepared, just once, to chance the moment and the toe? No, maybe death is a just a falsehood the lord has invented for fear of losing his labourers, she says. It's even possible his angels made it up themselves without his guidance. And what a fine deceit! If no one fears the world beyond the wall, everyone will leave. And then what will the angels do for sustenance and care? Angels are as helpless as a bush whose berries won't be picked and cooked except by human hands. A wing has never grasped a spade or worked a piece of dough or carried water from the well. They can't even lay an egg, can they? she asks, to shocked silence and then to laughter. What can an angel do without a little help, except expect to be obeyed? It's also possible, she finishes, that there is no lord above – Has anybody looked him in the face? – but only angels saying that there is. They claim to fly up to his firmament to tell him how his garden and his servants fare, when actually they only hide behind a cloud and then return with lies to tell and further orders for us to obey. We're pinned down in our orchards and our fields, she says, for fear of someone who's not real.

I'm still pinned down, Ebon thinks. Alone and pinned down in a thorny bush. He has to grimace at his new predicament but also at the memory of his escape from eden. He and Jamin must have made a sorry sight: the angel with his gimpy limb and the rope, hiding in the shadows of the barbican courtyard, the hooting of an attentive owl – You two, You two, I'm watching you – and Ebon himself, finally unshackled and with the blanket from his bed hanging round his shoulders, the very worst of capes. And then the comic, clumsy efforts of Jamin taking to the air again. Actually, though, escape turned out to be easier than expected, despite the over-hang. Thanks to a trusty angel and a trusty rope. And see the proof. He is there now, out in the world, just waiting and just shivering, uncertain what he ought to do and when. So far, so good, indeed.

Ebon does not need to form a plan. From now on, the world itself will command his every step. The light has lifted just a smudge. He is deciding whether he should break cover and try to blend in with the habitants of this cold place as if he were a newcomer from somewhere other than behind the garden wall or if it might be better to declare the truth at once, when a little dog discovers him. She is hoping for a rat, perhaps, or the chance to chase a cat. The smell is human, though, and not one that she knows or trusts. So this is Ebon's second certainty about the outside world. The first is frost and cold. The second is a growling dog, her chin pushed out, her little teeth alarming. The creature snaps at his ankles and his shoes.

Ebon's not been in the company of dogs before, though he has heard their barking from time to time, and he has pricked his ears at foxes in his orchard. So it's hard for him to tell if this is war or play. He has imagined that his best defence against the dangers of the world would be his human face and his speaking voice. His smile. He saw enough of the mortals when he was pushing alms through the barbican gates on fasting day to know that those outside had faces too, and speech. But this one? Well, she has a face of sorts. Her language, though, is just a pair of words, repeated endlessly, yack-yack, yack-yack, as subtle as a crow.

So Ebon offers her a smile and the usual words of greeting rather than a hand. But the dog is not to be placated. She is in a frenzy. It seems that she is calling out for help. He reaches down instinctively and fills his palm with little stones and soil. He throws them at the dog with all the strength and passion he has used when clodding the alms apple over the battlement just a few days ago. He is aghast, not because the animal has yelped and run away, evidently injured, and not because he is ashamed to have allowed his fear to express itself so spitefully, but because the hand he is holding up and inspecting in the semi-light is dark with soil and grazed with grit. So much for keeping clear of death. He has it now across his palm and underneath his fingernails. Ebon reaches down again but not for another fistful of soil. The dog has disappeared for the moment. He pulls his safety blanket from the ground and wraps it round his shoulders. If he's to die, he might as well be warm.

14

THE WINDOW SHUTTERS and the high oak doors of the greater masters' lodgings are still closed. It's barely dawn, but there are stirrings – some muttered matin prayers, wings stretched and exercised, the bill and coo of grooming. It's understood that at this half-lit time of the day nobody speaks until Jazib, the grandest of them all, signs that they can, but even then their voices should not be raised but reverential. They should not chatter yet amongst themselves but consider only their duties and fidelities.

There is some tension in the air because today a pair of them will be selected for the flight into the firmament where the lord of the garden can be found and where he will be waiting for the heralds to report on how the earthly heaven he has made for them has fared in harvest time and what they plan for winter and next year. Have they done well or disappointed him? He'll want to know if crops were plentiful and, if not, why they failed and what they might be planting for the coming spring. Green shoots, he'll declare, will not spring up from idle roots.

The two angel heralds will be happy to report a bumper crop, but hesitant to answer when he asks — as he nearly always does — if all is well amongst his habitants, his congregation on the ground. He seems to like those answers best. He'll want to hear of fellowship, community and routine, and then piety, discipline and work. Tell me that my devotees are settled and fed, he'll say. How could they not be when he provides for them plentiful and fertile grounds on which to pass eternity? They have such permanence and safety, such liberty from fear and want, such holy and enchanted lives, such happiness. He brightens at their gratitude.

He will not brighten much today when he is told about the unrest in the garden since the last report in midsummer when all was peaceable and well. Since then, the orchard-woman, Tabi, has abandoned them and gone beyond the lord's command, it seems. According to a trusted go-between, her fellow worker has plans to follow in her steps, with gemstones stolen from the bottom of their scripture chest, no doubt to be his riches in the outside world, where wealth is mightier than faith. And, more, this man has broken congregation handiworks, the devil in his arm. And filled his stomach with forbidden fruit. And spread discord in the lord's bright and ancient gardens. They have him shackled now with twine and ankleted with bells so every step he takes is heard, but there is still riot in the blessed air of eden. Its pot is cracked and leaking. How long before it empties out? The other habitants seem to have more sympathy for the punished malcontent than they have contempt for him and his sins. The orchardman is like the rotten apple in the pile. All the rest are softening because of him. A grub is digging its curly tunnels beneath their skin. One grub begets a thousand grubs, and then what chance for paradise?

Whichever pair of priestly angels is selected for the flight will have to ask the lord what further punishments are due for this string of disobedience. At best, it might be labour in the fields, a shovel and an endless mound of earth, an eternity of toil. At worst? Well, it is not unknown. It's happened once or twice before. A sinner simply disappears. The rotten apple is picked out and clodded high into the air, becomes a speck and then a star and then an emptiness. What's certain is that the smiling orchardman and the compelling orchard-woman, if she were to show her face again in holy ground, cannot expect forgiveness for their sins. The lord might not summon up a storm for them or impale their faithless hearts with shards of lightning. His anger will not turn the day to night. But he will want to know that order is restored and that the truants are entirely tamed.

So no angels are especially keen to be chosen for the flight today, despite the rare joys of spreading their wings about the firmament, twisting free as birds round unseen angles in the air and despite the splendours they'll encounter there, the nectars and the honeys they'll be fed, and the thrill of waiting on the lord in his own pious chambers. As dawn slips the thinnest slices of its light between the timbers of their lodgings, they do their best to huddle in the shadows, not wanting to be seen and then selected, not wanting to catch Jazib's eye. That mightiest of angels is still pondering. And worrying. What's happened at the end of harvest with the two orchard-workers cannot reflect well on his own authority or his standing with the lord, whom he fears as much as he reveres. The grandest angel should put an end to any disobedience before it even happens, he'll be told, and inflict his own authority and punishments. But he has failed in that, the lord is bound to think. Perhaps the time has come to pass his grandeur to a better, newer pair of wings, a different pecking order. So Jazib must be sure not to despatch a pair of angels who will impress and might be judged as good replacements for himself. But neither should he send a couple who cannot conduct themselves convincingly or are too overcome by being in the presence of the lord that they are careless with their choice of words. Jazib chits and chunters to himself, uncertain what the day might hold.

But then a gift arrives, a blessing in disguise, though not from heaven. The door bursts open suddenly and there's the go-between again, standing uninvited, exactly as he did a few evenings ago in the centre of the hay-deep floor, his body picked out in the slanting shards of the day's first light. This time the angels, though, do not affect to be asleep. They greet him, even. Call his name almost warmly. They hurry forward from their roosts and stare down at him, glad of the distraction. Whatever Alum wants – and, in his eyes, it is evidently urgent and important – is bound to delay Jazib's choice of heralds.

Their Alum's breathless, yet again. The man is always short of lung, it seems, when he comes through their doors. But he is also more dishevelled than they've ever seen him before. The wound across his nose, inflicted so amusingly the last time he was standing there, has healed but for a dark and narrow scab. Yet there are further, fresher wounds, across his cheeks and on his arms and hands, where thorns have torn at him. His familiar grey-green cloak is creased and muddied, and pocked with slubs of caught cloth. One of his legs is raw with nettle rash. And he is gabbling, even though he has not yet been given leave to speak. They pick up words and names but little more.

It's not until Jazib himself opens his great wings, flies down from the loft and lands as softly as a moth that Alum stops. Keep quiet, the angel says. Draw breath. He puts his face so close to Alum's that the go-between can look at only one eye at a time. Except he does not look. He drops his head onto his chest and tries to still his racing heart and heaving lungs. He seems soft and helpless once again. But when he lifts his head at last, after Jazib grants him leave to speak, he looks triumphant more than scared. His chin is firm. His eyes are proud. His voice is loud, and keen to give its news.

He has confronted sin, he says. He's ever vigilant. As he predicted there has been a plot devised, between the orchardman and – he hesitates; to name and blame an angel, any angel, is to take a risk – one of your noble brethren, the one who has command of fish.

And now his story tumbles out, with Alum as the loyal and plucky hero of the tale. In the darkness of the night and on the lord's behalf, he follows Ebon and Jamin down to the barbican. They are laden down with property, with valuables. He can only guess their purposes. But he stays hidden in the shadows until he sees what they intend to do. They mean to scale the sacred walls together and exchange the gardens for the world.

He does his duty, as his masters would expect. He reasons with them first, reminds them of their obligations and the law and warns them what will happen to their bodies and their souls should either of them touch first the lord's own masonry and then ill-fated soil. They will not listen to his words. Instead the angel Jamin takes to his wing as easily as any angel might. So much for his great wound. He's been pretending all along. He lifts the orchardman in his talons and flies him to the flat top of the battlement, though Alum does his best to bring them back to ground. He grabs hold of the fleeing angel by his feet. See here, he says to the gathered angels, pointing at his fresh scratches and his bruises. These are the wounds inflicted on me by Jamin. I managed, though, as they departed down the far side of the wall, to strike them both across their flanks with my cudgel and then to throw it after them. It struck Jamin again, I'm sure of it. If he had no broken wing before, he has one now. You can ask the keeper how I served you well. He witnessed it.

You broke that angel's wing? Jazib asks. I did, the go-between replies at once, or – he swallows hard – I might have done, it's possible . . . Too late, the question makes him wonder if he should have left that detail out. What greater violation could there be than a man clouting a master? But Jazib is evidently pleased. He turns towards the gathering above him in the lofts and laughs. We have a problem, do we not? he says to them. A worse one than I ever feared. An angel brother's flightless, or so our greatest hero, Alum, says. We have to thank our go-between for his great vigilance. He turns again towards the man and leans forward as if to kiss or whisper in his ear.

Today Jazib will fly up himself to the lord's firmament to break the latest news and make light of any disarray. No need to delegate the flight to other angels now. They will not know what story should be told. Let Alum who does not have a friend in eden take the blame for everything. For the missing orchard-hands. For driving them away with his unholy tempers. For any brief disharmony amongst the habitants, which he can guarantee will be restored once that rogue has been dismissed. For even setting upon one of the lord's own defenceless, blue-winged heralds. And let Jazib, the greatest angel of them all, be thanked for meeting his responsibilities and finding those at fault. A man who strikes an angel's flanks and breaks an angel's wing cannot expect to stay a trusted go-between. Let Alum, as the very least of penalties, be the one in bells and shackles for a while. So let him tinkle now, instead of squeak. And after that, if he's not clodded out of sight like a rotten apple, he can be given heavy work. In the latrines, perhaps. Or in the fields and pulling on a plough or – look at him, he already looks the part – a scarecrow in the mud.

Jazib is satisfied. His problem has been solved, thanks to the go-between. Yes, lord, he'll say, your order is restored, though at dreadful cost – an angel and two labourers. All three were seduced – or bullied, that's the truer word – to be the enemies of eden. We have the felon who's responsible and he is being punished in your fields. Your garden is a paradise regained. The greatest angel cannot help himself: he celebrates by taking flesh from Alum's nose again.

15

JAMIN STAYS LOW. He's lost some confidence in flying since his accident, though he has more stamina and spirit than he might expect, given how tired and flustered he is feeling. Those weeks of grounded rest, repairing in his bower at the water's edge where recently all his plumage has been groomed and then unbugged by Tabi's hand, may not have left him powerful but any damage to the ribbing of his wing has evidently healed sufficiently for more strenuous challenges than simply gaining the far bank of a stock pond or flapping to a wall-top with a rope. Now that he has had some days of stretching and testing them, his outer vanes have mostly flattened. He is lopsided, however, and has to compensate with uneven beats. It's still not elegant. He is the chicken rather than the dashing hawk he wants to be.

He is not in any danger, though. His encounter with the go-between at the barbican has been a shock, but the cudgel and the pisspot haven't done much harm. His

self-belief is bruised, perhaps, but little else. Nevertheless, for all that in his more heroic moods he might judge
himself a raptor, mighty and fierce-eyed and keen to hunt
for Ebon and the woman, he takes the cautious route and
flies along the summit of the wall, not trespassing beyond
it by even a wing-tip. His plan is to find a roost where he
can't be seen in the boughs of those great trees which
reach across the wall. He'll sit out the remnants of the
night and then, once the day is clear, disobey the rules
again by flying low or low enough to find and warn the
orchardman. He lets himself imagine, even, that he spots
the orange shawl of Tabi and that he flies the blanket of
his shadow over her until she stops and looks into the
sky. And there he'll be for her, a play of light and blue,
her saviour on a wing.

The flat bough that he has in mind – it's where he hurt
his wing in what seems an age ago – is not as undisturbed
as he remembers it. Someone has been there recently.
There are snapped twigs and shoe scuffs along the
branch. On the open ground below the tree he spots some
bark that's recently been dislodged and, just a step or two
away from that, several sturdy ivy swags, pulled loose. He
understands at once what they imply or thinks he does.
This has to be the route that Tabi took, when she broke
free. She must have used the ivy stems as rope. That's not
much of a challenge for an orchard-worker such as her,
who's as used to climbing trunks and scampering along

boughs as any squirrel. Then she will have dropped onto the wall and, after that, into the world.

It is a comfort to be sitting now where Tabi climbed and sat, he thinks. He snaps some twigs and claws the bark, just to add his marks of passage to her own. Those priestly angels might be glad to see the back of her, he thinks, but other plainer angels such as himself, other habitants, even go-betweens, will have been left with hollow hearts since she abandoned them.

He waits. The air will loosen soon. Then flying will be easier. Night air is like night water, turgid, chilly and unwelcoming. Sunlight lifts the body, though, and fills the wings. As soon as Jamin senses any warmth, he ventilates his feathers, tucks his wings in readiness, takes half a dozen steps along the flattened bough, his back turned against the only home he's known so far, and flies with appetite and confidence. He is an angel once again and not an earthbound fish-keeper, despised by all his brethren. He's purposeful, at last, and even masterful.

Jamin has almost forgotten how liberating it can feel to be so out of reach. He's low – hardly higher than the treetops – but still he's far enough above the mortal ground to believe he is untouchable and safe. At first he only concentrates on flying and finding where the streams and currents are in the fabrics of the sky, so that he can rest in them and take his bearings. But soon he dares to look below and start to understand the world. It's clearly not as rich and neat as eden or as well-ordered and designed. Other than the furrows in the occasional fields, there's hardly a straight line to be seen. He flies across a flattened, clothy landscape, stitched and woven, threaded through with paths and streams, embroidered with tall grasses and with trees, napped and textured with its hollows and its mounds, warped and wefted by its sinews and its rills. He's thrilled. He's brave. He's never been so full of hope before.

Jamin's misfortune is that he – unlike the jacks who live and die in Ebon and Tabi's orchard – has not yet discovered the demands of caution in the world beyond their boundaries. He's had no reason to. In Eden, angels always judge themselves invincible, as sacrosanct. All they have to fear is what the lord thinks and then might command. Alum and his cudgel were a deviation without precedent which could happen only if an angel tried to cross the wall, but never in the garden's holy grounds. But here, out here, beyond the battlement of eden, there are countless hazards to be fearful of, even for an angel. For there are boys with sticks and catapults and men with baited traps and snares. There's fire and pestilence and drought. But it is a hunter with a bow who brings the angel to the ground.

The man has risen early, as is usual on a hunting day. He means to walk down to the marshlands, a good distance from the hamlet where he lives. To reach the place by dawn, he has to leave when it is dark. He hopes there will be sufficient light from the full moon to walk quickly and with confidence. He wears his bow, slantwise, across his chest and back, and carries his best arrows and a knife. He's spent the evening stropping them. But at the last moment he decides to leave his dog behind. She enjoys retrieving any game he brings down for the pot, but he prefers to keep her bark at home where she can scare off strangers but not alarm the ducks and geese which are his prey.

He kisses his three children when he leaves, and strokes his wife, running the back of his finger against the nap of the hairs on her arm. She reaches out and touches his leg but is only half awake. She knows her husband will take care. She is allowed to sleep. She's pregnant with a fourth. She doesn't have the strength or energy to see him off with a wave. They have not eaten properly for several days. Now that summer's at its end, their rough diet – lately of roots, berries and hocks – is getting harder to forage. There will be acorns. Nettles are the last resort. The children look much older than their years, though they are small and bony. She has rashes on her cheeks and forehead and is weary. Even if their baby is brought softly from the womb and can draw breath, it will not have much mother's milk to suckle.

The husband is the hopeful, independent sort. He's not been tempted yet to be part of that rowdy throng who fight and jostle for scraps at the mystifying barbican and the gates that lead to . . . what? No one has ever been inside, even those foolhardy ones who imagine they can scale the wall, only to be beaten by the overhang. He himself can name at least three men who've broken legs or arms while falling from that battlement. He's heard talk of a neighbour's son who snapped his spine and died. That's not a risk the hunter has ever thought worth taking, despite living with the wall in open view each day of his life. Why snub your nose against a stone, when you can hurry unopposed down countless paths in numberless directions and not come to any harm? So no one he has spoken to has ever got any closer to the world within the wall than its great timber gates. They live with it as if it's hardly there because it hardly makes a difference. In fact, some folk advise it's best left as a mystery. Don't poke the beehive, they say. The honey isn't worth the stings.

So there might be a sunny palace behind those gates or even the shining paradise that minstrels sing about for all he knows. It certainly is not a place of woe or hardship, no matter what the darker stories claim. They're not short of food in there – or bells! – though it is only crusts, nubs and peelings that they offer in their alms each week. Some meagre charity! Some widow's spoon! A growing family won't survive on windfalls or stale bread. He can't help but wonder, though, what life must be like for those fortunates, on their side of the battlement, if bread is so abundant it can stale, and fruit is so plentiful it is allowed to sit and rot? By all reports, from what his neighbours say, when they have glimpsed a face behind the open gates, the cheeks are fat, the lips are greasy, and the people are all young. There's not a grey hair to be seen, or anything but smiles.

The man hopes tonight to look upon his family and see their greasy lips and smiles. At this time of the year, the skies at dawn are specked with skeins of geese and ducks which, on their way to some far places, fly too high for hunters, no matter how fleet their arrows are. But geese and ducks are bound to rest. He knows they spend their nights down by the marshes. All he has to do is to reach the birds before the air has loosened in the sun and it is warm enough for them to wake and fly. And get there earlier than anybody else. His arrows have to be the first.

It doesn't matter that it's cold, or that he has hardly any fat to protect him against the wind, or that his clothes are thin and worn. He's walking speedily. That keeps him warm. So does the prospect of the meal they'll have tonight. It's been a year since their last duck but still the taste of it lingers, the dark and smoky flesh flavoured with wild garlic and sage. Today he's hoping for a larger bird, a goose, or even two. Nobody ever gets a brace of duck. By the time the arrow has struck one, the rest have lumbered up and are on their way, bleating like a field of sheep or clacking like a tower full of bells. But geese are heavier and clumsier than ducks. They need to pound the water with their feet before they get aloft and, even then, their flights are shallow for long enough for a hunter with a steady hand to fire two arrows into them.

194

So this father has a dream that when he goes home he will at least be less hurried and less anxious than he is now on his way to the marshes. He'll have a cloak of heavy birds across his back, one for the pot tonight, to be shared with the old couple who eke out their final days in a nearby shack and – as is the custom – with any passing traveller, and another to be plucked and butchered, smoked and dried, for the winter. It'll help his wife stay strong for when the child is born. The dog will love the sinews and the skin.

The sky is scarcely silvery when he arrives. If there are birds, they can't be seen. They're staying silent. He must too. He treads as quietly as he can through soft and sodden ground, heading for the screen of rushes and reeds where he can hide and prepare himself. He squats and looks around, waiting for the moment when he might dare to push back the screen and draw his bow string. Some of the bog willows there have good straight suckers which could be fashioned into arrows. He'll cut some once he's got his birds, he thinks. He can fletch them with the feathers and wax their shafts with the goose fat in the evening. All he needs now is a stroke of luck, and light. He's anxious but he's happy too. And confident.

Indeed, there is a host of birds floating in the marshland's lakes and meres. Though the hunter still cannot see a single one, he can hear their cries. A grey and chilling mist has settled in, hugging the ground, though hardly damping down the honking of the geese, the quacking of the ducks, and the calls of winter fowl that he can recognize and name without even seeing them. All he can watch, in the brightening skies above the mist, are unruly gulls, contesting scraps of fish, and a single heron, laborious in flight. He knows he must be patient. The mist will burn off fairly soon. It will be fine and sunny, though too late, possibly. Those plump birds might all be gone before the view is clear. He'll have to go back to his wife and family, clutching willow suckers but with nothing better for their suppers than, perhaps, some hand-caught frogs or watercress.

The intervention of the mist is almost more than he can bear. He knows it isn't wise to move or make the slightest sound, but caution means an empty pot. He readies his bow, pushes through the reeds and wades into the water, trying his best to sound no larger than a coot. It's possible the mist is clinging only to the shores and that the deeper parts are already warming in the sun. And it is so. Before he is waist wet, his face is struck by sunlight. He has to squint – it's blinding him – to see if there are any birds within range. But he dare not lift a hand to rub his eyes. Instead, he turns slowly in the water, making hardly a ripple, and puts the sun behind him. There's movement in the reeds not far from where he's standing, though that might be just voles, which no one wants to eat. If there are birds, they're bound to show themselves, betray themselves to him in time.

He is practised with his archery. Within a moment and with the daintiest of movements, he has slotted the nock of one of his arrows into the string and snugged it up against the belly of the bow. He draws a sturdy length, holds steady on the flight and waits. His heart is shaky, but his hands are not.

It is by instinct rather than design that when he hears the angel flying overhead, coming from behind with wing-beats heavier than a heron's or even a swan's, the hunter swivels on his hips, points his arrow roughly at the shape and lets it fly. The whoosh is from the bow string and from the breath which he has held but now releases from his lungs. He hears the thud of contact and puncture before he has a chance to see and name what he has shot or even wonder at its majesty. This is something he can't recognize, a vagrant swept in by a storm, perhaps, from some distant place. He's never seen a bird so glossy and so blue before, or one so large. His own son is not as big as this. Nor his wife, even with the child she's carrying. Its wingspan is three strides across at least. It's not a graceful flier, though, despite its size and grandeur. It's obvious, as it attempts to get away, forlornly seeking footing in the air by ladling what little breeze there is, that, even before the arrow struck, this bird was injured on one side. But, no matter. Ungainly meat will still come sweet and sticky from the pot.

That single arrow isn't enough. It hasn't brought the bird crashing into the marsh where it can be dragged ashore and finished off with fist and foot. It's persevering with its flight, but it is already slow and weakening, more meat than bird. So there is a chance to lodge and point another arrow and, even, to take time perfecting its direction. But the fletching on this arrow is not well aligned and so the hunter's second shot strikes short. It just glances the coverts in the creature's undertail and sinks into the plump flesh below its vent.

There is no need for any further arrow, though. The blue bird drops into the water with such a splash that any of its wider, smaller kind that can either hear or see rise up at once in their alarm and speed away. The sky above the mist is briefly ripe with finches, warblers, grebe and coot, with chats and jacks and gulls, and with duck, with swans, with geese. Their cries of danger, Stay Away, are piercing and unmusical. Then the sky has nothing in it but the sun.

The hunter has to wade out into the water up to his armpits to get a good grip on the bird. It's quite a sight – the sky-blue plumage and the spreading bloom of blood. There is some twitching in a wing and leg, and there's a heartbeat still. But when he holds the bird's great head under water for as long as it takes to – as a kindness – end its misery, there is hardly any fighting back. Very quickly, there is none.

It would be sensible to let the bird bleed out into the water and then drag it into the reeds to pluck it and to butcher it right there. But then no one will trust his word when he describes the weight of it, the colour and the span, the sheer splendour, its improbability, when all he has to show as evidence is meat and giblets. He can imagine how his two daughters and the boy will gasp when they set eyes on what he's brought for them. Besides, he's curious to know what his ancient neighbours will say about the bird. They might have seen its kind before and can share its name and how it is best prepared. Is this one for the pot or for the flame? Should any meat left over be preserved in salt or pickle or in herbs or only dried in lengths and left to hang?

So he starts to pull the corpse ashore. It's easy to manage in the deeper water, as it floats. In the shallows, it is bulkier and heavier. It takes all his might to land the bird fully and roll it onto a flat bed of reeds where it can drip and dry. He sits beside it on the cushion of plants and drips and dries himself. The mist has lifted, shifted, and the sun is smiling down on both of them. Well, he thinks, chuckling at his own good fortune, thank heaven that I haven't got a brace of these.

Now that the water has drained off, the body weighs a little less and can be carried. It might appear as bulky as a growing son or wife but, like all birds, its skeleton is flimsy. Its feathers hardly add much weight. The hunter can lift it onto his shoulders, though not quite as easily as he can hoist his two lively, living daughters and carry them from dawn to dust without tiring. He has to sink down onto the ground beside the bird and sort of wrap himself inside its wings before struggling to his feet. He can't imagine what he must look like. Will he appear, when he gets home, more like a clown than the best of hunters? Let them think what they want. Out there, alone and with no witnesses, he feels magnificent, a feathered emperor with meat enough to make his family fat. My father would be proud of me, he thinks.

The return takes longer than the going out. There is no urgency, so long as he stays clear of any passers-by who might be tempted to demand some of his catch for their own pots. He is seen and stared at, as he walks. Cottagers come to their doors and shake their heads in puzzlement or disbelief. What great blue thing is that across his back? They've never even seen a harvest sky that blue, let alone a bird. A dog investigates, too baffled to bark, its nose wet with curiosity. Some giggling children come too close, thinking they might snatch a feather for themselves. He has to shout at them. He has to shake off flies.

Not far from the path that leads up to the hamlet where he lives, he is intrigued to see a body climbing in the ancient oak tree where there's a disused hunting hide from those lost days when deer were plentiful but now is only used by children as a den. A woman he has never seen before, wearing a striking orange woven shawl not quite concealing her amongst the first autumn leaves, is standing in the crown as comfortably as a jack or squirrel might. He braces his legs and squares his shoulders as best he can for this stranger and cannot help but try to catch her eye. He knows he is a rare, astounding sight in his heavy feather cape. She can't have seen before, wherever she is from, a hunter more victorious than him. He even deviates a step or two to the side just to pass a little closer to her den, so that she might see more easily his bounty from above.

He half expects her to descend. Then he can use their conversation as an excuse to stop and rest. This is a truly heavy bird. But, instead of calling out with the wonder and respect he deserves when he draws close, she shouts at him, as mad and gabbling as any lunatic. He hides his face from her – it's for the best – and hurries on under her high perch, his curiosity about the stranger replaced by sudden fear and – oddly – some embarrassment. This woman is the sort, he suspects, who'll pelt him with acorns or dead wood or send down curses on his head. But she only stands up in the branches and continues to cry out. He hears the rising torment and the horror in her voice.

He's encountered such suffering before, but never from a woman. Once, when he was a greenhorn with a bow, he put an arrow in a deer in failing light. Instead of finishing the job, he stood too long, admiring his first shot. So before he had the sense to fire a fatal second, the animal escaped into the woods to die. The young huntsman never managed to find his prey, despite his father telling him not to come home without meat and arrow.

The undergrowth was far too thick and disobliging for him to track them down. But he had to listen helplessly to the animal's agony all through the night until finally, at dawn, its blood ran dry. Then the silence that it made was thunderous, as was his father when his son returned empty-handed. The greenhorn had only himself to blame.

And now his own blood's running dry and cold. He's unaccountably ashamed, despite his triumph in the marshlands with the mighty bird. He's hoped to never hear again so sad a sound as that departing deer. And he has not. Until today. The woman in the branches of the tree is to his ears a cornered creature at the end of hope and time. But the hunter will not stop to speak or offer any help. He's weary now. He has a family to feed.

16

EBON IS A wary man who understands he must be cautious when he's taking risks. He will not leave his cold and stony hollow in the thicket until the sun has cleared the trees and there are other people, busy in the unkempt lanes and fields and yards, amongst whom it might be possible to pass undiscovered. Stepping out at dawn would only draw attention to himself. Although he's never been a stranger until this morning, he knows as if by some buried instinct that the half-lit stranger is more suspect in this world than one who comes by day. His face has always been familiar and named in eden. But show it here, in shadow, before the sun reveals its own familiar face and he might be challenged, asked his business, wondered at by folk less easy to deter than one small dog.

Ebon has wiped the soil and grit off his hands as best he can, using only grass and dew. He knows that when he picked up and threw the palmful of stones at that ankle-snapper, he thereby squandered his immunity from death. But he feels exactly as he always feels at this time of the day: a little stiff, a little tired, but nothing sinister. He has more than half expected to be a shaking leaf by now or, at least, to sense death's shadow passing over him like autumn and robbing him of colour and of sap. The angels' sermons always promise fear and pain for any habitant defiant enough to touch unholy ground. Yet Tabi, clearly, was not afraid of that. Or believed it, even. It is a comfort to remind himself again of her relentless doubts. The masters tell us that, she said after one wet and punishing day of labour in the orchard, to keep us tied to this. If her certainty had made her brave, Ebon had better share her disbelief, for the moment anyway, if he's to find the courage that the day demands of him.

Being slow and careful, though, will not help Ebon if he is to rescue his orchard-woman in so brief a time. He has only till sunset, just one working day. No, he cannot wait until the sun has cleared the trees, whatever caution says. He has to be as reckless as the woman herself. He can't imagine she will have hidden away in some damp hollow, fearful of the day. She hasn't left the garden just to hide like he is hiding now.

He ducks out from underneath his thorns, shakes himself as he might do each morning at his own bedside, pulls the blanket tightly round his shoulders, and steps into the half-light. He looks around, interpreting the shapes and silhouettes and waiting for the world to send a sign to him and offer invitations. The first evidence of daily life he recognizes is smoke, a twisting strap of it, ghosting from the straw roof of a hut and flecked with orange embers, a short walk across a muddy field. It is fresh planted with spring wheat, thinly but untidily. The tilth is claggy and pocked with yellow stones which have worked their way to the surface. If he were home, he'd feel obliged to dip and start to clear them as he walks. The second sign – as soon as he has dared to start his trespass in the field – is that small dog again. She isn't growling now but yapping, warning anyone inside the hut that there are strangers on their land. Yet no one comes, and finally the dog tires of her own noise and tries something new and inexplicable. She wags her begging tail. The creature's only skin and bones and hair.

It isn't until Ebon has crossed the field – with just one yellow stone in his hand, lifted as a token of an estate more painstaking than this, but also as a warning to the dog – and is standing at the hut's rough door and coughing from the smoke and from anxiety that the sacking is pulled aside and a face peers out, uncertain whether it ought to be alarmed or welcoming. It's a woman, though her features seem male. She looks the stranger up and down. She sees a man in costly clothes that appear slept in but with a damp and dirty blanket hanging from his shoulders. He has no beard. He has no lines. His skin is lustrous. In these deep, infertile backsoils of the world where people are allowed to squat and live on land that no one owns or wants, it's rare to see a stranger such as this, someone who hasn't come either to sell or to buy or to take advantage of their innocence but just to wander in and out at will. No doubt, in those estates and cities she has heard described as crowding out the rich valleys beyond their forests, plains and hills, there are ten thousand men like him who have the time and wealth to do exactly as they want. But here, the to and fro is less dramatic and less leisurely. A man who has to worry in his life, like every son and husband that she knows, could never stay as fresh-faced as this stranger. His good looks make him menacing and less than human, she decides. And he has a boulder hidden in his palm. She flaps her hand behind her back to warn her children to stay quiet and out of sight. She stretches out her other arm but can't quite reach the bludgeon that her husband always leaves propped up for her behind the door when he's away from home. Still, she has her knees and fists, and she can bite if this unblemished fellow tries to bother her. What is it, then? she asks.

Is it unwise to tell the truth? Ebon sits down, at her bidding, on the flattened tree trunk outside the woman's hut, while she searches for something for her visitor to eat and drink, as she knows she must. She's bloated round her stomach as if she has a great gourd beneath her apron, but she is as thin and gawky as a twig elsewhere. Her face seems worn and tired. Her skin is dry and lustreless, but she is dramatic to the eye in ways that Ebon has rarely found before in his gardens on the safe side of the barbican. She is like Tabi in some ways – the same chestnut hair, the same sharp face, the same blue irises – though barked and rusted by the wind. Her manner is not spirited but doe-like and suspicious, more tabitha than Tabi ever is. She will not sit beside him on the log as normal manners might dictate – at least in eden – even when he drops his rock as if it is as harmless as a leaf and pushes it away with his shoe a little sheepishly, but instead hovers at the hut's door, ready to retreat inside if the stranger comes too close, ready to retrieve the bludgeon and strike him first across his knees and then, when he is down and fool enough to try to rise, across the head.

It is for Ebon, though, an almost overwhelming thrill and oddity to converse with someone new, with someone whom he has not met ten thousand times before and worn thin with daily greetings and old news. She is his first stranger, and he is embarrassed to find himself so bashful and so keen to charm her and persuade her he is safe. He hardly recognizes himself while they exchange their clumsy pleasantries across the hut's untidy yard. Today he sounds as ill at ease and unconvincing as Alum does when pretending to be a good neighbour. He cannot find his natural voice. He only hears himself – as if from afar – talking as stiffly as an angel might converse with any underling. He does not mean to condescend but cannot help himself. Speaking with outsiders is not a skill he's ever been called upon to use.

The breakfast that she offers Ebon when she returns is last night's pan bread and a drop of water. He's eaten only blackberries since yesterday and was hoping for something warm and filling. One of his fasting days is more packed with taste than what she hands him. But he is wise enough to finish it and to pretend that a cup of cloudy water is a treat and thin black bread a feast. When he hands back the empty cup and grins his thanks, she lifts her head and offers him a timid, satisfying smile. The world outside is not so scary after all, he thinks. The people are sweetly shy, like robins, hesitant and curious and brave. He settles back onto the log, glad of the chance to rest and talk and form a plan. What is it you are wanting, then? she asks again. At last. Who are you looking for? She might just as well have said, Why are you up and out and in our yard at this time of the day when decent folk are busy with their families?

It is a pleasure to describe his orchard-woman to her, how bright and lithe she is, how memorable and striking in her orange shawl. She wove that shawl herself, he explains, in the colours of an autumn leaf. The woman shakes her head. No, she's not seen anyone like that, not once, not in her thirty years. Nor has she ever seen so fine a shawl. Who are her people? she enquires. What's her family name? What village were you living in? She hopes to send him somewhere else.

Ebon tells the woman where both he himself and the missing Tabi have come from. Behind the wall, he says, and can't help but grin again with pride. He lets his hands describe the outline of the barbican. Have you been there for – He stops before he mentions charity or alms. He knows those bags of rinds and scraps and his baskets of mushy windfalls barely merit being called charity. But, yes, she nods. She knows about the barbican. She waves her own hand now and points. It isn't far from here, she means. But no, she shakes her head and tuts at the very thought, she has never taken alms up at those gates. Her husband is too proud for that. He thinks the givings might be cursed or laced with poison of some kind. That would explain the sicknesses her neighbours suffer from. Their swellings and their blisters, the shivers and the flux, the cough that lasts a hundred days. It's said that people there are yoked like oxen to their ploughs or fenced in like sheep in a fold. She shrugs. What business can it be of hers or any of her neighbours'?

Her visitor cannot conceal his bewilderment. Curses? Poisons? Sickness? Yokes? He can't imagine how the sunny cloistered gardens of his home could produce such fear and fantasy outside. So he describes for her the life he leads within the great circle of the wall and how the alms are given not with malice but with love. He talks about the orchard and the nuttery; the hives, the stock pond and the wells; the barns, the granary, the bakery; the fields, the meadows and the glebes; the laden tables that they have, their fasting days, their feasts. She looks at him in wonder and then with disbelief and then with scornful suspicion as she gathers from his answers that his garden has no husbands and no wives, no children and no ageing, no death, no hunger – so he says – and no want for anything except the blessings of their lord. It has angels too! They fly to heaven when they choose. You might have seen the shimmer of their wings, he says. And what of dragons breathing fire? she asks, not scornfully exactly but impatiently, and . . . She tries to think of other creatures she has never seen but heard described in stories and in song . . . spirits, gremlins, devils, walking trees, people with two noses and a single eye? He laughs out loud. No, none of those. He understands she's mocking him now. Trust me, a tree cannot have legs, he starts. But lets his sentence hang unfinished.

She has been dutiful if not entirely welcoming, but her mood has changed. She has a life to lead. Now she is clearly wanting Ebon to leave. This man might be courteous and fine-set and probably not dangerous, despite that yellow rock, but he is not a person she should trust. She keeps on looking out across the raggy field of wheat as if she's half expecting someone to arrive and save her from this visitor and all the lies that he is telling her. She whistles for her little dog to come and snarl again. My husband will be home quite soon, she says, defensively. He went out hunting for a duck. Armed with his bow. But, no, she can't invite this stranger to sit at their table and share the meal. She already has too many mouths to feed. See, she says, and points towards the door of her hut, where, unnoticed up till now, and standing as still and skinny as three sticks, her son and two daughters are listening. Her visitor is startled more than makes any sense to her. It is as if he's seen the very creatures he has denied just a moment ago, the devils and the walking trees, the half-blind and the double-nosed.

Ebon, indeed, is so shocked he takes a backward step. So these are children? he enquires. She shakes her head again. This man's a total fool. Possessed, perhaps. He surely can't be drunk. It's far too early in the day. Yet his mouth and eyes are gaping wide with wonder, like some madman encountering a butterfly for the first time and looking as likely to tear off its wings as burst into tears at its frailty and beauty. Before he has a chance to step towards the door to peer more closely, even touch the children, their mother tells them sharply, Go back inside, you lot. And then, to Ebon, Yes, I might have seen the woman you talk about. She cannot look him in the eye when she's deceiving him. I've seen somebody with a crimson shawl like that. An orange shawl, he corrects her. That's exactly what I saw, she says, it was an orange shawl. As orange as an autumn leaf. She points at once across the brow of the hill, towards the barbican. There is always a little crowd up there, she tells him. I hear that sometimes food is lobbed across the wall. She might be one of those who hope to feed on it. She'll be there now.

Ebon knows that he is being invited to leave and not only by the little dog. He wishes his encounters at her door had been less awkward and more elegant. He'd like to stay there for a while and try again. But the phrase, She'll be there now, has worked its trick. There is no time for lingering. He thanks her, as he must, and hurries off. The people of the world are strange, he thinks. Their warmth is hesitant, their welcomes distrustful. He knows he has been clumsy and misunderstood. But, now that he is alone and striding out into a land that's bright with light at last, it isn't long before his spirits lift again. He reaches the summit of the little rise beyond the hut from where the woman said the wall of eden could be seen and, sooner than he has expected, he looks down towards the familiar and reassuring outline of the barbican. He can just make out and hear a crowd of people gathered there but they are still too far away to tell if there are any orange shawls.

The woman's dog is snarling when Ebon leaves their little yard, but her snarling turns to yapping as soon as he is out of sight. She's glad to see the back of him. Besides, she's spotted someone else, her master coming home, wearing a blue cloak of feathers across his shoulders and she can smell bird flesh and expect a day of cracking open bones and feasting on its giblets.

17

THE FIRST TO discover the two rope ends dangling from the wall into the hollows below is a boy who's been sent off by his parents to scavenge snails for the family pot in the salty crevasses of the stonework. He's excited by his find, although its meaning is unclear – except that for any child an unexpected rope is bound to be an invitation to climb up, despite the warnings he has heard and the challenges above. The parents and a group of their neighbours hurry over when he calls, slowing only to step round the mud and puddles in the wide but shallow moat below the wall. They gather in the day's first glints of light, peer closely at the boy's discovery and shake their heads, as wisely as they can, glad to start the day with something to discuss. The rope ends have been newly cut, it seems. One daredevil has the nerve to pull on one length to test its strength. The other length lifts up, goes almost out of reach. The tallest man amongst them has to jump and level it again. It's clearly just a single stretch of rope looped round a cop.

The wall has always seemed unscalable, impassable, and so they've learnt to pay it hardly any heed. The best it offers them is snails. In busy lives, what can't be done should not be pondered on. Except at night. When they are gathered round their hearths, they're bound to scare themselves with tales. Then the grounds beyond the barbican are full of ogres, imps and ghosts that dwell in moonlit palaces, or with imbeciles and cannibals who feast on bats and children. Who'd climb a wall to keep such company? They couldn't climb it anyway, not with that jutting overhang, that thrusting chin of masonry. But, at last, there is a way to conquer it, a rope, though no one dares to scale the wall just yet. What lies beyond presents too great a risk or, at least, too great a mystery. They might very well discover the moonlit palaces from stories and then be met — and devoured — by those imps and brutes. But, honestly, all that anybody truly knows is that anything is possible, but most things are unlikely.

Now the mystery deepens. One of the women finds a long and well-made cudgel that has been left and probably forgotten by someone in the grass below the wall. It has a blue cloth grip wrapped around its handle and is fancier than anything they've used themselves. No one claims ownership — or forgetfulness. But it's worth keeping, that's for sure. She swings it round her head, playfully, almost dislodging her green scarf. This'll keep my husband in his place, she says, to laughter from the other women, who know her husband all too well. Still, they can't make any sense of what they've found. A cudgel and a length of rope? What story could be fashioned out of these?

The first to try to scale the wall is the boy who found the rope and therefore counts it as his own. He means to show off to his cousins and his friends. He regrets it half-way up because the fibres are rough and tear the skin on his young hands. They are unstable too. He cannot shift his weight from one arm to the other because the rope is slippery and only loosely looped. It shifts from side to side each time he tugs on it. You have to use your legs as well, they tell him from below. But he hasn't got the strength or – now that he is bleeding – the will to perse-vere. Besides, he's reached the shadow of the overhang. The stone is damp and slippery with moss. And he is stuck. There is no way to get around so bulky an impedi-ment. He doesn't have the muscles or the reach. The best that he can do is to bang his head and blunt his elbows on the stone. Whoever built this wall has built it well. The boy has to bounce and slither down again, to jeers.

Now an older man – his uncle – though no less of a braggart, muscles forward to show the boy how a wall should be climbed and can be climbed without drawing blood. He gets a couple of his brothers to secure one end of the rope and take the strain while he coils the other round his waist. Now all he has to do is to call out Pull

and he can walk up . . . well, spider up . . . loosening and
tightening as he braces his legs against the masonry. It's
not as simple as he'd hoped. The rope slips up from his
waist onto his chest and is so tight that, every time his
fellows step back and pull, his ribs are crushed and he
can barely breathe. Even if he were to call out Stop or
Lower me, the pressure on his heart and lungs would not
ease until he reached the ground again. And then – in fair
proportion to his age and boastfulness – he would have
to deal with even louder jeers than those suffered by his
nephew, especially when it's spotted that he too has cut
his palms. So he grins and bears it, determined not to fail
or fall. The overhang is almost more than he can manage,
though, even with the rope. But he's a tall man and has
sufficient reach. He pushes himself clear of the under-
eave until he is hanging from his rope like an ivy swag.
After three or four attempts and the sweating certainty
that, from below, he must look like a fool, he manages to
grip the top edge of the masonry. If he's not quick, he'll
either fall or hang himself. Powered now by fear as much
as muscle, he hauls himself – chest first – over the cops
and onto the flat pavings below.

The uncle's all but disappeared. No one can see him
from the ground. He's lying face down on the summit,
waiting for his heart and lungs to still. This is his reward
for showing off. It's only when his brothers anxiously
yell his name that he stands and displays himself. He
raises his arms – with both hands clenched in fists to

hide the blood – in self-regarding and self-mocking triumph. He is a hero, for the moment anyway.

What now? His family and neighbours are asking him
to describe what he can see. They've no idea what to expect, but, now that they have somebody – their very first,
their pioneer – up on the wall and within sight and smell
and hearing of the truth, they're hoping that there is
nothing they should fear. All the stories they have told
themselves when they have gathered round their fires and
heard the night wind beating on the barbican and shaking its great gates have never truly been believed but have
nevertheless always had a tighter hold on them in the
darkness than any daylight logic ever could. A yarn that's
spun and woven out of midnight flames is always stronger
than the silks of day. But standing in the shadow of the
wall this morning they have their fingers crossed that fire-
side stories don't come true and that the world beyond
the wall will turn out to be not so very different from
their own. Something dull and unremarkable would not
be a surprise. After all, the great trees that reach out
across the rampart are no different from the branches that
reach in. The birds that come and go across the wall – the
pies, the jacks, the peckers and the tits, the rooks and
starlings, and the doves – are all familiar. As are the
plumes of smoke when winter fires are lit. As are the
many bells they hear from time to time. The plain likelihood is that, as those winged creatures who live on either
side of the wall must share the daylight and the stars, the

same winds and the rain, those people who dwell within are similar as well, just families who do their best to eat and work, to sleep and love, to live as free as air.

Their hero for the day is not a man of great imagination. He is not tempted to invent for them a land of palaces and gold, or one of ice and snow demons, or even tease them with his sightings of, say, fish with legs or dragons breathing fire. He does, though, now that he can breathe again and has a calmer heart, recognize and like the status he has gained simply by standing on the wall. He is the fount of knowledge suddenly. He'll be plainspoken, honest and dependable. He just describes what he can see: an empty courtyard, wider than a field and fringed with tarbonies, but paved with shining, brindled stone and swept clean of everything, including footsteps. On either flank there's woodland and some scrub, just like the woodland and the scrub they have outside, except cut squarely and in rows. There's a trim and perfect pathway leading off, enticingly. And, no, there's not a sign of anybody there or any voices either. And, no, there's nothing to be frightened of, as far as he can tell. And, no, he doesn't want to scramble down, just yet. Or won't admit to it. He thinks, though, that he can see, below a line of firs, the roofs of buildings at the far end of the path, though they are grander and more ornate than the barns and homes they know on their side of the wall. Instead of thatch and laths, there's tile and brickwork, a belfry, possibly, and chimney pots.

Now, shush! I see people, he says, shielding his eyes from the expanding light. There's some excitement in his voice at last. He can just make out a work party of habitants. They're wearing almost identical pale smocks as if all their clothes have been made by the same mother. They are crossing the trim and perfect path on what must be another path, though narrower. They're walking single file, like geese, he says. He's nervous suddenly. He's trespassing and can be seen. He's now the tallest cop on the wall. These distant figures are something plainer and more disturbing even than imps or ogres. They're armed with tools. He can see the metal glistening. He squats down on the wall top and shuffles along to make himself invisible behind the masonry. He is jeered by all the upturned faces at the foot of the wall. Stand up, man, they call out. Let yourself be seen. Show them you are not afraid. They're more scared of us or ought to be, one woman says, dramatically, not really knowing what she means. The woman with the cudgel swings it once again. And so the temper of the day is set.

The hero, hiding behind the battlement, regrets that he has volunteered to conquer the wall. There can be no going back for him, unless he wants to be the poltroon in the story they might tell for years to come. He wishes he was not alone up there but could haul up someone after him. It's easy for the groundlings to be brave. It's hard to be courageous when you are standing – squatting, even – with no company to share in your alarm. I'll let you in, he

219

says. See for yourselves. It can't be hard to open up those gates.

His brothers secure one end of the dangling rope again, glad to be part of a drama rather than just setting off, as they would normally at this time of the day, to hunt or glean, to forage or fish, or simply take their hunger for a long and unrewarded walk. He hauls up the loose end and lets it drop and dangle into the courtyard. He has no plan except to get down from the wall and retain his dignity. There is no chin or overhang defending the inner face of the wall and so it's quick and easy to descend, although his hands are still tacky with blood. Before there's time to hesitate, he plants his feet on paving stones on hallowed ground. He cannot help but whoop with triumph to let his friends and neighbours on the far side know that he's the bravest and the first. It won't be long before he's tackled all the bolts and bars of the gates and can welcome them inside as well.

The whoop's been heard by the people in the work party. They stand and point at him, not sure what they are witnessing or what they are required to do. At first, they wonder if the man who's evidently climbed down their wall – there is a dangling rope – and is now tugging at the gate bolts is the gatekeeper, the only worker who has leave, for duty's sake, to touch the masonry. He must just be doing maintenance or whatever he's devised to make him seem less idle than everyone knows him to be. There's no one idler, except the angels. And the go-between, perhaps. But then the keeper himself appears from his little guardroom where he lives and sleeps. He's angry, evidently, shouting at the man, stepping forward, raising his short arms. He is not used to being so disturbed, especially so soon after that strange, alarming fracas before dawn with the stock-pond angel and the go-between. It is an outrage that anyone should even touch his gates. He is the only one who has ever been allowed to slip their bolts, swing their hinges and crack open their timbers. He wags his finger at the man. Once the fellow turns and shows his face, so he can be recognized and named, he should expect a reprimand if not for trying to escape into the world then, at least, for being disrespectful to the barbican. He can be reported first to Alum and, thereby, to the angels themselves. He reaches up to pull the fellow by his ears.

A shocking thing occurs. The man the gardeners do not recognize steps away from the hinges and the bolts, swings a fist and knocks the keeper to the ground. They can hear the slap of his body as it hits the paving stones. And then, before he has a chance to rise, the stranger delivers a second practised blow to the keeper's chin with his foot, and then a further two into his chest. Even Alum wouldn't dare to use such violence, with witnesses. The victim rolls onto his back, jerks a little and then is still. The hero of the day, stoked up by everything that has occurred, is tempted to deliver one more blow. The keeper's face is known to him. He's glimpsed it through the gates several times at the far end of those hazel stales at almsgiving, pushing out derisive gifts of slops and swill. And he's hated it, even as he's jostled forward to collect a share. But he can bide his time for that final kick against the keeper's inviting chest. What he must do at once is to let his neighbours in.

The gardeners are mystified, though not frightened yet. All they can express amongst themselves is shock and bafflement. If only they were quicker off their marks, they could run down to the barbican to help their brother and take hold of his attacker before the gates are opened out. Think what a story they would have to tell that night. And, afterwards, their everlasting lives might carry on as normal. But they are frozen to their spots, like rabbits. They have no idea how to oppose a stranger who can use his feet and fists like that. Nobody knows what they should do other than be timid witnesses, that is until a sister volunteers to run back to the roosts and let one of the angels learn that . . . that something strange is happening and that the other masters ought to know. Once she has gone, her companions edge a little further down the path, half sensing that they must at least appear to mean to aid the gatekeeper. It's tempting to stay far away but also tempting to get closer for a better view. They've almost reached the safe side of the courtyard, where the tall trees grow and provide the camouflage of shade, when the barbican's great timber gates are opened up and the world comes crowding in.

The second incomer they see is an untamed woman, fascinating to the eye, with a green headscarf and holding a cudgel in her hands, a cudgel that they think they recognize: Alum has had a tool like that of late, and with the same blue grip wound around its handle. All this is Alum's doing, they think. Quite soon there are a dozen others at her shoulders, then a whole host more, spreading out below the barbican, as uncertain what to do as the gardeners themselves. There are little people too, strange to behold, and spindly ones, as grey as ice, and suddenly a dog. It is the only creature there that dares to occupy the middle ground. It stands alone in the centre of the courtyard, simultaneously barking at those on the far side and wagging its tail at all its friends behind. Both groups might well decide to stand there, gaping at each other, until the sun goes down again, such is their indecision and their sense that something far too large is happening . . .

. . . except that the keeper has now recovered sufficiently from his winding and his bruising to stand up and do his best to hobble away from his abuser and the throng towards his fellow habitants. Their instinct — better late than never — is to hurry forward themselves to offer him a helping hand. The instinct of the throng, now that the circle has been broken, is to follow him across the courtyard, to let him lead the way. They gather at his back, bunched up, impatient that he is so slow but unwilling to overtake so small and halt a man and put themselves in danger. What is certain is that everything they see is strange: the lifeless neatness of the courtyard, the straightness of the paths, the ruly gang of labourers in their dull uniforms and with their ageless, polished faces. What is uncertain is what will happen next. Given such strangeness, the incomers will not be surprised by anything, whether it be an army of archers and spear carriers or some ancient hospitality, the offering of smiles and hands to shake, the giving out of food.

But not one of the work party imagines for a moment that their visitors mean well. They witnessed the way the gatekeeper was struck and kicked. They hear the snarling of the dog and see its teeth. The woman with the headscarf and the cudgel can be seen amongst the crowd, as can the man who has the feet and fists. His hands are bloody too. So tools are raised up in defence and then, when that does not appear to make a difference – the keeper and the horde are getting closer by the step – the more timid of the gardeners peel away from the back and, half crouching and half scampering, disappear into the undergrowth. It takes only a heartbeat for the others to do the same. Except they run in full. Some of them even drop their sickles and their spades. They know where to hide until the angels come, as come they must, to impose the lord's eternal peace again. This is the moment when the people of the earth, now seeing no one in their path who might oppose them, find the courage, finally, to shove the limping gatekeeper forward in front of them as a living shield. If there are any dogs ahead or men with bows, let the teeth or arrows bury into him. They shuffle forward into eden. So it all ends, and so it all begins.

The sister who ran off to carry news of this invasion to the angels meets, by chance, with Alum first. He's coming through the oaken doors of the greater angels' lofts. A figure of authority in normal times, commanding and precise, he is this morning hardly recognizable to her. His cloak is torn and muddied, his legs and arms are scratched, and when at last he takes his hand away from his face he reveals a new and still bloody wound across the bridge of his nose.

The gardener screeches out her warning but the go-between seems deaf to it. He looks in shock, as if he is already aware that there are strangers at the gates and is, indeed, the victim of their punches and their cuts, but angry too. He's muttering beneath his breath and cursing like a devil might. Whatever's passed inside the loft and might have happened at the barbican has left the go-between battered, breathless and alarmed, alarmed enough to fear eden more than he has feared the world. The sister repeats herself and finally gets a response and – after a moment of thought, during which the angels' man seems to rejuvenate and brighten – a decision. The masters do not need to be disturbed at this time of the morning, Alum says. Let them rest in peace. Leave everything to me. I'll go down to the barbican myself.

Except he does not go down to the barbican. He only

seems to for a hundred steps while she is watching him. Those steps last long enough for him to calculate what he can do to save himself from the lord's and angels' wrath. He sees the fear and panic of the working party as those who are not hiding in the undergrowth come running up the path towards him, shouting out that there's a mob of mortal maniacs not far behind. They've got your cudgel, someone shouts accusingly, as they run past. And another, They've got dogs.

It is the sight of the gatekeeper, struggling towards him with blood running down his neck and blossoming across his shirt and with a throng of untamed strangers at his shoulders, that persuades the go-between that the prophecies were true, that Death itself will come to punish them, if the lord is betrayed by any disobedience. There is no future anyway for Alum in that place. He might as well be dead or dying. Eternity has turned its feathered back on him. He knows the angels are no longer his. That second wound across his nose has marked his final fall from grace. He has no friends amongst the habitants and never has. There's nobody to bid farewell to. That much is clear. But those pairs of escapees, that Adam and his Eve, that Tabi and her orchardman, might hold his future in their hands. They were the wise ones, it appears. They reached the world before the world reached them.

Alum knows exactly what to do. He does not wait to help the hobbling keeper or to argue with the crowd. He swivels on his feet to face the hub of buildings and he runs, like he has never run before, driven forward less by fear than by an opportunity. He'll go first to the dormitory, ignoring anyone who asks, What's going on? What should we do? It doesn't take him long to find a sufficient length of rope and then the satchel underneath the bed where he has stored the things he values most, not least the purse of coloured stones. He helps himself to someone's leather hat, and someone else's sturdy boots and a good stout walking stick as he returns to the dormitory door, yelling at any fellows who block his path to move aside or feel the stick. He will not stop to talk to anyone about the panic in the air. Too late now, is all he says. Though what he means by that, they cannot tell. Quite soon he's reached the holy spaces and has retrieved the shiny, ornamented knife that he discovered what seems an age ago and the silver chalices and censers from the prayer room aumbries. Now, at a trot, he follows down the path which takes him to the almost open ground, where he still pictures Ebon, his one-time enemy, smashing up his barrow and his trug and spilling chaos onto sacred ground. He slows only once he has reached the shadow of the trees. He's heading for the ivy swags, the flattened bough, the summit of the wall, the rope, the drop, the landing and the moat, and then the open promise of the world.

18

TABI HAS FOUND a tree-cabin in which to pass her nights in safety. She supposes, from the drawings of deer and wild goats scratched onto its laths, that it was built for hunting, but it has clearly been neglected and disused for many seasons. The only evidence of recent life is that brought in by squirrels and by the shitlegs who in their hundreds come to roost and leave their lime and berry traces on the cabin's roof. She chooses to believe that if the cabin wasn't always meant for her to find some sanctuary, it was at least her destiny to happen on it. She can sit inside, on her bed of gathered straw, and watch the world pass by in all its odd variety. She is surprised – and a bit ashamed – to recognize how being free has left her more hesitant than she ever was in eden. She'd thought by now she would be rubbing shoulders in the company of strangers, sharing their tables and their conversations. Instead she is finally living up to her name and is as edgy as a tabitha, furtive, hidden, waiting for her chance, though partly hoping it will never come. Only when she is more used to this new land will she descend, will she join in.

Her flight from eden was sudden but inevitable. An overladen twig might only snap and fall in its own time, but it is bound to snap and fall eventually. On that night when, wearing just her sleeping shift, she sat outside the dormitory in the resined awnings of the fir trees – it seems like only yesterday – she felt the cold for the first time since the spring. And she recognized its prompting. Unless she acted quickly, the winter would close in on her and her spirit would lose all its leaves, her sap would freeze, her anger, boredom and restlessness – even the many blessings of her life – would become more burdensome each day. Then what? Another spring, seed time, fresh buds and work. And after that, as sure as night will shadow day, another harvest and another fall of leaves. More of the same than she could bear.

She had been irritated but then glad when Ebon found her squatting underneath the firs. His body close to hers could help to stop her shivering. She took the chance, when he pulled her to her feet, to squeeze his hand. Surely he must have known her well enough to understand what she was telling him but dare not say out loud. Stay well, sweet Ebon, and farewell. At once, she felt as if she owed it to the man to keep her word, or at least to keep the promise of that squeeze. She'd let him down and betray herself if she could not devise a way to migrate with the swallows and the swifts and discover what it was that made their wing-beats resolute.

Now in the awnings of another tree, beyond the wall of eden, Tabi cannot but wonder at her luck. Without it she might still be in the custody of firs. Getting out was never going to be a simple challenge, even though she was not daunted by any garden rules: you cannot trespass where you do not sleep or eat or work; you must not touch the holy wall; you cannot chance a finger or a toe unless you mean to die. Such warnings did not count for much when weighed against her longing to be free and startled in the outside world, whatever it might hold.

On the morning after squeezing Ebon's hand, she dressed warmly in her orange shawl, filled her pockets with some breakfast leavings and set out. She hoped she'd not be missed until she didn't show up for the meal that evening. Ebon would very probably believe that she was spending a second day resting her injured fingers at the stock pond. Jamin was not expecting her, although he might be hoping she'd favour him and his eels above the orchard trees. Alum was busy, squeaking around amongst the other gardeners. She simply walked down the tended and permitted paths towards the barbican, as if she had a message or a purpose. What could seem more innocent? Once there, she'd slip away into the undergrowth and hope to find some footholds in the sacred masonry or, better still, a tree to help her with the climb.

She'd heard there was a dip in the battlement with branches stretching over it. She'd search for those.

But good fortune smiled on her. It was madly generous. If she had not spotted entirely by chance that the great gates of the barbican had been left slightly open for a moment while the keeper went inside to fetch some oil for his weekly greasing of the bolts and hinges, she might not have felt invited to go forward across the courtyard and then tempted to peek out. But, once there, she cannot have been thinking clearly. She only meant to see what she could see. It did not occur to her at once simply to slip outside through the open, liberating gates, though the opportunity was blindingly apparent. It must have seemed too easy, too unadventurous, not brave enough, she tells herself, baffled by her own bone-headedness. Her mind was still fixed on a climb. Indeed, it's possible, though foolish beyond measure, she now realizes, that she might have turned away altogether and carried on with her first plan of lizarding the wall if she had not heard the keeper coming back. Caught in the moment, it seemed obvious at last that she should take that single step between the hardly open gates and disappear at once rather than let him catch her there and suffer his chastisements and his seizing of her arms. Then she would have to bear whatever further punishments the go-between might inflict when he got word of what she'd tried to do.

She'd felt hardly any fear of sudden death as she stood

with her back against the gates but instead an unaccustomed lightness to her shoulders. Even her injured hand seemed more flexible and healed than it had done just moments earlier. Her horizons had expanded suddenly. And so easily. What had the never-ending fuss been all about? It was spine-tingling, actually, not just the novelty of this new place seen from the banned side of the barbican but the instinct that, from this day forward, her eyes would dance at everything they saw. And there was a satisfying bonus too: she'd finally chanced upon some way to undermine Alum's standing with the angels but without having even touched the lordly mason's sacred wall. Such good fortune was an omen, wasn't it?

If Tabi wondered at all whether or not she'd been too hasty at the gates in those first few moments of free will, the sound of the keeper pushing shut his newly oiled bolts with her outside was all the prompting she required. She bent to touch the alms slate for good luck and crossed the wooden bridge and moat into the world. She might as well. There was no going back for her.

For the moment, though, she is determined to stay hidden in her tree cabin. She longs for company and misses some of those she's left behind, their chatter and their bickering, their close interest in her daily life, her regard for theirs. She certainly is missing meals and bed. Once or twice since her escape she's woken in the middle of the night and stretched her hand out expecting, in her fuddlement, for it to land on flesh, not straw. With every day, though, she is getting more resigned to being on her own and talking only to herself. There are no bells to tell her what to do or any angels reproaching her or bearing orders: be modest, do not overeat, no hammering, no hastening, don't sleep too late or take tomatoes from the vine, and leave those apples on the ground to rot, be humble, frugal and restrained. Just not to work is reward enough for flying out of eden's coop. She can sleep all day if that is what she wants. Or tell herself the story that she hopes her eden brethren will hear in time, the tale of three thrilling absentees, Adam, Eve and Tabi. Or simply sit and wait for that moment, which will come, when she can start her life again – and face up to its ending.

Each evening, when she can walk unnoticed and unchallenged, she dares to foray into fields and villages, seeking food and water and peeking into stables, huts and homes, as nosy as a cat but just as heedful too. She draws back into the shadows, hardly breathing, if anyone comes close or looks out in her direction. She does not stray too near to lights or fires or open doors. She keeps well clear of cats and dogs, though has to wonder at their utterings and smells. What is surprising is she never sees a table like the one in eden, with everybody gathered round and sharing pots and jars and talk as one community. They always eat their food inside their own small rooms, as far as she can tell. Some of them even eat alone, as silent as their candles.

The first few times she ventures out, she finds it hard

to get back to her cabin. She is not used to walking in the dark, nor to not knowing exactly where she is without the reassurance of eden's modest size, its latticing of perfect paths and its familiar scenery of smells and sounds. This world's unpatterned and unplanned. But she soon learns to turn around as she heads off, to check how different her journey back will look compared to her going out, how no two sides of anything are matching, how the wind upon her cheek provides the clue to which direction she should take and then reverse for coming home, how moon and stars can help as well.

Tabi is a seasoned food thief. She has become well practised in the lord's estate with the deceiving dip-and-take of scrumping. A little curtsy at the knees, while there is no one there to notice her, and she could have in a split moment, too speedily even to break her stride, a radish or a pea-pod or a vine tomato in her hand and another in her apron pouch for later in the evening. And then a third. Straight in her mouth. Well, they taste better taken secretly than washed and trimmed and tamed by cooks.

So she looks forward to her evening raids, although she quickly learns that, just as in the lord's estate, harvest's at an end out here. Search though she might, she has not yet discovered any fresh vegetables or even fruit to steal. She makes do on scraps and slops left out for animals, except on one occasion, when she reaches through a window and makes off with a cooling pot of stew. It scorches her hands and then her tongue. She has to eat it with her fingers and then spoon up the gravy with a leaf. She cannot know that she has tasted meat. Of course, she misses the restful, loving suppers she enjoyed with her fellow gardeners in eden, but there are richer feasts outside. There is the feast of knowing she is free, the feast of sleeping on her own, without a single snorting neighbour, the feast of laziness. Already her hands, which always have been rough and splintered from clambering, are softening. And she can feel her muscles getting stiffer, though that might be the ageing that angels warn about. Every little twinge of pain, every tiny splutter of her gut, every yawn or sneeze or cough, might mature and prove true the angels' prophecies.

But, actually, for all these worries about death, it feels that time is standing still rather than reducing. Mortality, if it exists, is not as hurried as she feared. Unlike her sisters and brothers in eden, where all the time is allocated, spoken for, the people whom she spies on at night through their lamplit windows and their open doors seem to have all the time in the world. They don't behave as if they're running out of it. Nevertheless, she is not tempted just yet to make her own days pass quickly. She will squat like a raven on its twiggy nest and enjoy the leisure and this chance to learn the world afresh.

The more that Tabi sees, the more reluctant she becomes to be a part of it. Everything is stranger – more outlandish, even – than any nightmare she has had or any dream. What might at first seem everyday turns out to be a shifting drama in their hands, a dance, a mime, a show of laughter, then of tears. Everything's a good excuse to share what they are feeling. She's never heard such shouting or seen such animated faces. People seem to touch each other all the time. And they are so often purposeless. If she ever joins their flock, she fears she'll be a duck amongst the hens, and pecked for being different. She asks herself – again, again – why am I so confused by them? Why stepping back instead of going forward?

Her questions do not have any answers yet, but by just asking them of herself – sometimes out loud, as if she is reciting prayers – they help her to understand the contradictions of the world, the sweet and sour she has witnessed from her hideaway. She wonders at its troubles and its joyfulness; its screeching children and its wagging dogs; its chaos, grime and disarray; its laxity, its daily grind, its hand-to-mouth; its gaiety and hardship; its heartache, heartbreak and its joy. She takes some comfort in her unaccustomed solitude from the casual cheerfulness she overhears, the gossip and the arguments, the time-wasting, the acts of kindliness, the ruthless jokes and teasing. It is as if by witnessing, she's also taking part but staying safe. The garden never was as loose and carefree as the world on this side of the wall or as embroidered. Its cloth was always cut as plain as possible. Whatever brute or blackguard made this place, it certainly was not the same lord who fashioned eden. That lord would never be so whimsical and fickle. Compared to this, his paradise has been begotten endless, sullen, constant, dull, sedate.

She has witnessed from her secret hideaway a baffling stream of passers-by: there have been lovers walking hand in hand, and girls with sticks, directing goats or sheep, and groups of men, all talking but not listening, and women dressed as if the weather doesn't tell them what to wear. The greatest marvel and a shock has been the sight of people knocked about by time, their faces drawn and lined, their bodies as gnarled and twisted as any ancient tree, their heads as silvered as a fish. A stocky man goes by, leading a horse and an open cart, containing pumpkins and a wife. When he returns in the afternoon, he is alone and riding. She wonders what might have happened to the woman and the cart and what will happen to the vegetables, until at last she understands: this is what the world is all about. It's wondering and stories. Now she has a way to entertain herself each moment of the day. She has only to watch and hear a body passing by and she can invent their lives. Back in the garden, all was known. The future was the past. Nothing was a mystery. There were no stories to be told except the ones that preached obedience. Perhaps one evening in the time ahead she'll have the chance to tell her sisters and her brothers in the garden what she has seen and heard.

Only once, on her third day, is she discovered in her tree. A small boy tries to climb it while his parents are talking for too long with another family. She sees him staring up at her, and she remains silent, unsure of how to deal with him or what to say. He must have hoped to claim the high hut as his own while the conversation stretched out, but there would be no point if an adult was already there. He scrambles down and starts tugging at his mother's hand, eager to move on. It is touching that he turns to look at her again, before they leave. She hardly waves to him — just lifts a wrist — her first and modest contact with their world. O, how she wishes she could take his hand. O, what she'd give to wake with Ebon at her side.

On the morning of her sixth day, she observes a corpse — so what the angels say is true, to some extent — or at least the head and feet of it. The rest is wrapped inside a white cloth and being carried on a stretcher board by four stone-faced men, amongst a party of a dozen snuffling mourners, two of them with spades. They rest beneath her tree for a while, and Tabi can peer between the branches to look death in the eye, or in the face at least. The eyes are covered with a pair of shiny stones. But otherwise she might mistake the body for a sleeping and untroubled man. She waits to see his fingers twitch or for his chest to rise or for his mouth to part for air. But he outplays her in that game. He holds his breath eternally. When they move on, the wailing starts again.

Such shaking grief, she's never seen before. What must it be like to expect to die and so to live with knowing it, to sleep with it, to wake with it? Why are they not in constant fright? What are they feeling when they weep? After almost two weeks here, she still does not know.

One morning, before dawn, she hears the hunter whistling tunelessly and hurrying towards her on his way to the marshes. She wonders about the bow across his back. Perhaps he means to climb her tree and occupy the cabin, hoping for some game. She would not mind it if he caught her eye, just as the small boy has. He is a handsome man, she thinks, though not quite as tall or set as Ebon is, perhaps. His smile might brighten her and give her reason, finally, to speak with someone other than herself. What once was solitude is fast becoming loneliness. But he does not even pause or look up into the branches where he might have seen her staring down. He hurries on with more skip and spring in his step than she has seen in any of her sisters or her brothers when they set off for work — save Ebon, perhaps, the tree-lover. She allows herself to wonder for a while if the bowman might turn out to be a friend.

At mid-morning, not so very long since he last passed by, she listens to the man again, returning, though much more slowly than before. She means to let him see her in the branches of the tree. It is a risk, she knows, but something in the lively way he's walked and whistled in the morning has made her count him as a brother. There is

239

no sign of any skip or spring in his return, however. Nor is he whistling. This time he trudges slowly towards her tree cabin, grunting from his efforts. It is not until he has almost reached the spread of her oak that she can look down on his burden. She stands between the two supporting boughs outside her cabin, meaning only to wait until he's close and then to draw attention to herself. It's her turn to whistle. But now it's not a man that holds her eye. It's something wider, longer, feathered, blue.

Tabi does not breathe, let alone whistle. She is at once so winded and so dazed, it is a wonder she does not topple from her tree and crash down at the huntsman's feet. She has to steady herself against the cabin. In less time than it takes to blink, her body goes from ice to fire and back again. Then for a further moment, also as fleeting as it's infinite, she is as numb as that man on the stretcher with his stony eyes. Her heart has stopped, as if it's lost the will to beat. She's sagging at the knees. What has she seen? A wounded creature being hauled to safety? That is too much to hope for. An angel walking to her in the world, with a mortal strapped across his chest? A hunter with an angel for a cloak? Some spectral fume of fancy that has survived her dreams and come to taunt her in the day?

Tabi's heart has shocked to life again but is now racing. And she's faint. She should lie down. Certainly, she is unwise to lean out from her branch, over such a high and giddy drop, to better see what she must hope never to see again. But she has to be quite sure of it. And, no, this is no chimera or just the tricked-up blue of sunlight on some shiny sack. O, let it be so, but it's not. She cannot merely shake her head to make it disappear, although she tries a dozen times. She's certain now. This body has no life. The swarm of feeding flies is evidence of that, as are the streaks of drying blood across the hunter's shirt and arms, as is the way the head is lolling heavy from its neck, like the loose cloth noggin of a doll. Still, she waits to see if any feathers twitch. But the body outplays her in that game. It will hold its breath eternally. And it's Jamin.

If her stomach were not empty, Tabi would throw up. She shuts her eyes as tightly as she can, hoping that when she opens them again, she will come round as if from a nightmare. The only angel she has liked and cared about is dead. She's massaged that skew-whiff wing herself, and recently. She's pressed her nose into that nape and almost kissed. She's loosened blood-black ticks from off his rump and fed them to his fish. Her touch has had him purling like a dove. But now, if he's as lifeless as he looks, everything she's ever known about the world is false. If angels can be killed and hefted round like sacks of grain, she thinks, nothing in the world is safe or good.

Tabi knows who has to bear the blame. Reproach already thuds against her chest. This blue body is her punishment for blasphemy. The lord can work in cruel and unexpected ways. How has she ever imagined that if

241

she ran from eden, she could outpace his wrath? Her Jamin would surely not have flown from the garden with his half-broken wing had she not blundered out herself, for what? Revenge? To satisfy an arrogant and selfish yearning? To be surprised and startled by the new? To have the freedom to pick apples off the ground and bite them to the core? Her stock-pond master must have come to save and rescue her and paid a shocking price for so great a tenderness. Her escapade has been a cruel mistake, a vanity. She'd only meant to escape eden and its masters, not to injure it, not to import mortality into its cloisters and its lofts, not to slay an angel.

Her stomach and her chest convulse. She shudders from the grip of it and cannot stop herself from screaming out in despair and pain. She knows the man below has noticed her standing there, high in the branches of her tree. He's almost slowed, in fact, as if he means to talk to her, to pass the time of day. She yells again but consciously this time. She means to be both seen and heard. But hers are cries of anguish, not words that carry any sense, any more than the starlings – now shaken from their roosts and shrieking and screeching along with her in the oak's high crown – can speak to men with meaning. There are no words that can express the anger and the shame she feels. The moth in her that has desired the moon is now the wolf that can only howl at it and make no difference. And so she howls. She is a wounded animal, pierced by the arrows of a brutal world, a world that is too cruel for this one fragile innocent to bear.

The hunter's pierced and shaken too but mostly baffled. He turns, despite the burden on his back, and stares into the branches of the tree until he can't avoid her eyes. And he is stung and shocked by them as if by a hornet. If her cries were frightening, the torment on her face is worse. She's like a creature from another world, untamed and inconsolable, one of those hellcats he has heard about but never met before. Such women are beyond help, he tells himself at once, hoping for the least excuse to flee. The devil has them as his own. Let him take care of her. And so he dips and hides his face and hastens on, away from Tabi and her grief, towards his wife and family. This encounter's shameful, though. He'll keep it to himself.

Tabi will not fall silent until he has reached the brow of the hill and, legs first, goes out of sight. The last she sees of him and of Jamin is a distant shimmering of blue. She is determined for a coldly conscious moment to descend – to crash down from the tree – and pursue the feathers and the man. Her fists can hammer down on him until he is as bloody as Jamin. She'll splinter him to smithereens. But her legs and arms have, for the moment, lost their bones. She can hardly stand, let alone run. And so she lets her fists hammer down instead on the tree trunk, pummelling it with all the anger she can muster until both wrists and hands are hurting even more than when Alum twisted back her fingers to retrieve the tomatoes she had stolen. The patterns of the bark are imprinted in the soft parts of her palms, and there is blood. And so finally, sobered by the pain, she sinks down onto the floor of the cabin and, coming coldly to her senses as if waking from the most exhausting dream, draws in deep breaths to still her racing heart, her damaged hands, the panic in her lungs. So this is precious liberty. Jamin has paid for it. Now Tabi must atone with something more than bloody hands. O, lord, forgive her for her sins.

If Tabi has to compensate, she cannot do so from the safety of the oak. She'll have to let the starlings reclaim her cabin for themselves and go back, hang-shouldered, to the place where she is known and where she is accountable. She can't avoid the truth of it. Retracing steps will be the punishment for her deadly selfishness. There is a sacred wall that she must climb and then a holy garden to embrace again, and then a heavy door to push aside into the angels' loft where she must speak and share the weightiest of words. She has a sudden image of herself. She's face down on the hay-deep floor. The priestly angels are all gathered round. Her brothers and her sisters have assembled too. She's flattened there by guilt, regret and shame, feelings she has not experienced in eden. These are her gifts, her heavy trophies from unholy grounds.

Her eyes are watering. Here is another stream that never dries and is as old as life itself. Here is another endless flow, a sour and a salty one.

THERE IS HAVOC in the air when, finally, Tabi finds the strength and the resolve to descend from her tree. She's expecting to be challenged as a stranger once she is in the daylight of the world. In fact, she doesn't earn a second glance from any passer-by, despite the brightness of her shawl and despite the torment on her face and hands. The lanes and paths are much busier than usual. It is as if a bell has sounded, calling everyone to hurry up and meet. They are expected. She follows, doing what she can to walk like them, with purpose and with eagerness. She is not surprised entirely when she finds the place that everyone is heading for is where she was bound to head herself, the open ground on their side of the barbican and just an apple's throw away, across the moat, from eden itself. She's hoped never to see its battlement again, but now she has to enter it somehow. She can't suppose the keeper will oblige for a second time by oiling his great gates.

The gates are open, though, more widely than she's ever seen before, certainly more widely than the meagre gap allowed for oiling. The broadest wagon could get through or Four Horsemen, riding side by side, their saddlebags packed with sword and famine, beast and plague.

It's an alarming, rowdy sight. All sorts of folk – a greater gathering than there's ever been by anyone's account on almsgiving days, even in the dead of winter when food is scarce and hardship at its bluntest – are crossing the wooden bridge, passing below the barbican's battlement and spreading out across the inner court with mischief in their steps. Again, she has no doubt who has to bear the blame for this calamity. Because of her these worldly siblings must have gathered in a multitude and stormed the gates of eden. An angel's taken from the sky, so chaos will unfold, just as surely as thunder follows lightning. These are the fruits of disobedience and all its bitter woes, its uproar and its pandemonium.

Tabi stands apart and just watches, unsure of what she has or even wants to do, as the multitude thins out and empties into eden. She feels what Ebon briefly felt at the last almsgiving when he looked out into the world for the first time: that she is seeing animals in rags. There is the pumpkin-carter, reunited with his wife. There is the mother of the tugging boy. There is the ancient with the strident voice. There are the lovers, though no longer holding hands. There are the pallbearers. There are many strangers too. Strangers to her, at least. She can ignore them all. They can never be her brethren. But there is one who catches her eye and will not let it break free. Three children and a plump-waisted woman – heavy with a swelling, it would seem, and so not wanting to be jostled in a crowd – are also waiting just a few steps back, behind the shoulders of her man. She is wearing a tall bonnet made of felt and with a single feather protruding from its band. Angelic blue, and freshly plucked. Tabi doesn't need to wait for the man to turn and show his face. She knows already who it is and what she wants to do.

She hurries forward, dodging through the few remaining onlookers, those who are too old or frail to risk a new experience. Despite her still bloody and throbbing hands, she means at least to knock the bonnet off the woman's head and reclaim the feather. That swelling's begging to be punched, as well. Then she will turn her rage towards the man. Flesh on flesh, at last. She'll do what Alum did to her. She'll bend his fingers back until they snap. She'll bend them back until her own wrists snap and cramp again. Let them both – the hunter and the orchard-girl – share in the pain that Jamin must have felt. What will happen afterwards, even if those animals all turn on her, she neither knows nor cares. But because her body is too drained, she takes too long. The rear end of the crowd has closed in round the barbican gates. By the time she reaches the back of it, the woman and her family have entered the inner courtyard and are walking off excitedly to see what they can find. And what they find almost at once – or, at least, her small boy does – makes the family seem more human and more innocent again in Tabi's eyes. It is a string of shiny wether bells that somebody has either hidden or discarded. Such pretty things. He jiggles and tinkles his treasures all the

247

way along the path until – hoping, sensing, he is being watched – he turns and sees the woman in the orange shawl not far behind. He shakes his bells for her and, in return, she hardly waves for him but just relaxes her fists and spreads her fingers as if she's letting go the pain that she's inflicted on herself and would inflict on them. It is her second and disarming contact with a child. He can, together with his family, proceed, untroubled and unbruised, towards the beating heart of eden. And that's a kind of miracle.

So far the only lasting damage done has been to the gatekeeper. Since his felling and his kicking at the barbican, the intruders – in their hundreds possibly – have been too astounded by their ventures and discoveries to do much more than gape and touch and smell. Mostly they are being drawn along the paved and tended paths through the gardens towards the pavilions by the firs. Their progress will be slow because everything they see is new and fascinating, not just the neatly tended beds of winter vegetables or the few remaining red strigs of berries in the soft-fruit enclosures – which very soon they've tasted for themselves, their faces smudged with earth and juice – but also the method and the process of the place, the spacing and the patterns and the shapes. It does not seem possible that such an ordered world has rubbed its shoulders for so long against the near side of that wall, while on the other side brute nature, mayhem, ruled the roost. Compared to where they've spent their lives, this place is paradise. For the moment, they're respecting it.

For Tabi, though, the sights are hardly fresh. She's walked these paths before, ten thousand times in living memory and countless times beyond recall. Her steps today, though, are weightier than they have ever been before. Her legs are tree trunks and her heart's a log. She has betrayed eden thrice over, first by abandoning this blessed place, then by luring Jamin to his slaughter and finally by coming back to it and bringing havoc with her. It's peaceful for the moment, yes – but high spirits and bewilderment are bound to turn to recklessness and callousness and greed. Outside the wall, when she was biding her time in her tree cabin, she was hidden but alive. Inside the wall today and burdened rather than lightened by her longed-for loss of innocence, it feels as if she's in a dream, invisible and airy, no longer flesh and blood but like some bitter curse, a bane. She barely dares to lift her head. She recognizes many faces, though – her one-time brothers and her sisters, her fellow toilers in the orchards and the fields – but they seem just as dazed as her. If they are surprised to see her face or even recognize her – has she changed since her escape; might she look older even, coarsened by the world? – they are not showing it. No one gives her any greeting. No one offers an embrace. She might as well be just another stranger, come to rip their lives apart.

Tabi knows this is no time to throw herself onto the

249

angels' hay-deep floor, weighed down by her regrets. That moment's come and gone and taken eden with it. Instead, she ought to – and she might as well for all the difference it will make – turn around and leave at once, back to the barbican, back to the world. The garden that she knew is being poked and prodded; soon it will be widdershinned. It cannot judge or punish her. Her sins are insignificant. She doesn't matter any more. She turns again but hesitates. There's something she must do before she passes through the gates again. Go back to her orchard. Smell and taste it one more time. If there's a single apple left on any of the trees, she will plunge her teeth into its flesh. She has, she knows, been happy working with those trees, despite the life of rules and bells, more happy – no, less troubled – than she'll ever be again, for sure. She hopes to find and recognize herself, the person that she was and wanted to escape from, the person who sat so recently in Jamin's bower with his feathers in her hand, the fearless woman in the canopy staring beyond its branches and out across the wall with hope. Will they remember her, the trees? Will his fish remember Jamin, now he's gone? Will the orchard and its falling leaves forgive her for her sins?

One or two lost souls from the world are picking through the fallen fruit when she arrives and are either eating what they can or salvaging those apples and those pears which are still whole enough to store. A man is beating walnuts from the trees with a length of fallen wood. A little dog is barking at a bush, hoping to flush out a bird or animal to chase. Tabi almost stumbles on the mound of freshly broken earth where the jack was buried many days ago. It wasn't there when she last worked in the orchard. She wonders what the mound might signify. Another death? She bends and finds herself a fallen apple amongst the scoundrels and the scamps now hidden in the leaf litter. She's not had a scrap to eat today. The flesh is bruised and cottony. She perseveres with it and strips it to the core. Her stomach hunger is replaced by hunger of the heart.

19

As soon as he reaches the barbican and its flung-open gates and sees the loop of Jamin's rope tied round a battlement but with one end hanging on the mortal side of the wall, Ebon guesses broadly what must have happened. For a while he is loath to return to eden. He can hear, far off, the hubbub of a crowd. He crosses the timber bridge and stands by the almsgiving slate outside the great gates and peers into the now deserted courtyard. Its normally swept and shiny stone is scuffed with footprints and littered with leaves. There is what looks like blood outside the keeper's room. And dog waste too. He twists around and looks out into the vastness of the world, but it is just as deserted there. It is as though it's emptied itself into the gardens and he's the only person left alive outside the wall. But, no, there is another person, striding along the ridge about an apple's throw away. That figure is familiar but it is only for an instant that Ebon lets himself imagine it is Tabi, and that he hasn't failed. He's found her after all. But all too soon he recognizes that short man – and almost hears the usual squeak that once accompanied him. It's Alum heading out into the world from where he must have crossed the wall, a loaded satchel on his back, a walking stick, prepared for anything and with that bounce in his step that marks a man who is not fearful of what lies ahead but, rather, keen to blunder into it.

Ebon's still polite, a decent and forgiving man, despite the defeats of his day away from home, despite the bells and tethering. He lifts his hand to wave. Old habits must die hard. He does not, though, quite dare or even want to lift his voice and call. The angels' man is already out of hearing and he will soon be out of sight along a winding and uneven track which stretches now beyond the power of his eyes and might never end. No matter where he finishes, the world will always want a go-between.

Ebon will not follow him – for duty calls. O to be an angel and possess the gift of flight, he cannot help but think, though hardly for the first time in his life. At least for angels it is simple. A stormy rush of air, that's all, and they can soar in their blue cloaks of feather into the skies above the garden to know what's going on and not be part of it. But he is earthbound and must remain a grounded man. That is the dull and soily truth. So, at last, like everybody else this morning, he walks into eden through the yawning gates, across the courtyard and up into the gardens, heading for the row of firs where he and Tabi last touched hands. Quite soon, the paths are busy and unruly with uninvited visitors. It's satisfying to discover, halfway there, the same small boy he spotted earlier hidden in the shadows of his mother's clothes and the sacking at the doorway of their cottage. He's found the string of little bells which only yesterday were Ebon's shackles and is making something hopeful, something cheerful, out of what was punishing. Otherwise the orchardman encounters mostly lawlessness. What started as a trickle of trespassers – the woman with the cudgel, the hero of the day, the jeered-at boy who couldn't scale the wall – has become a jostle and a crowd and then a throng. They do not mean to run around in such disarray or shove each other impatiently, but the moment must be seized by them or else it will be taken by others. They trespass into barns and granaries, wander through the smithy and the warming room, rummage in the cellars and the wash-house, pillage in the kitchens and the bakery. There's not a door that isn't opened up or a drawer or cupboard that isn't emptied out and sorted through. There's not a bed that isn't turned and searched or a larder that isn't stripped of food. They are amazed by what they find and what they decide to keep. Even the stock pond is invaded. Fishing there is easier than it has ever been outside. One man has scooped up a plump carp in his hat. Another has herded an eel into the shallows, where it struggles, gasping for air amongst the reeds, before it is grabbed and left to writhe inside a bag.

So Ebon's tempted, when he witnesses marauders dragging stored potatoes and turnips from the winter clamps, with scant regard for any damage they cause, and tugging next year's cabbages and herbs out of the soil by their roots, to remind them as calmly as he can that there is bound to be a price to pay for theft, even if it is the theft of food for hungry mouths. And when he meets people coming back along the path with their arms full of the bedding and clothes they've taken from the dormitory, he has to resist the impulse to seize them back. The same with stolen pots and pans, and jars of honey, pickles, oils. But he stays quiet. Their guilt cannot compare with his.

Ebon doesn't really care about the few belongings by his bed. If they are pilfered, so what? He does care, though, about his trees. He's left them for only a day but already they are missed and reaching out their boughs for him. And so he never goes back to the firs or to the bed and table where he's slept for ever and a day but turns instead towards the orchard he has always loved. Quite soon he is amongst his trees and he is glad – yes, glad enough to spark some tears – to hear what he takes to be a greeting from the jacks that have found refuge in the canopy. He gave one of them a noble burial. They're thanking him, he thinks. The jacks must be the only creatures left in eden who will be thankful for anything he's done.

But, for all the mayhem taking hold in this once safe

and sacred realm and all the burdens he is shouldering, there is some bliss awaiting him on what has been, so far, a hellish day. It is the orange shawl that he sees first, from a distance. Someone has stolen it, he thinks, and has the nerve to wear it where Tabi used to work. Then, for a moment, he imagines she is lying dead somewhere and whoever now has got the shawl only pulled it off the shoulders of a corpse. No question, he will take it back, reclaim it for himself, just for the chance of smelling her again. But with every forward step he takes, the orange shawl grows larger, as does the hope and then the suspicion and then the certainty that the orchard-woman has returned. And, yes – he's joyous, overcome; his heart is pounding like a bird's – it is his Tabi waiting there. Expecting him, he thinks. He slows down and walks more carefully towards her turned back. He wants to touch her first, before she sees his face. She has a windfall in her hand. As usual. But now she won't be punished for her sin of biting it. One thing's for sure, no angels' man will seize her by her wrists.

Tabi feels the weight of Ebon's hand on her shoulder but hardly has a chance to turn and smile. She isn't startled by the touch and sight of him. She always knew she would be found if she returned and if not found amongst their trees, then where? But, for the moment, her attentions are taken up elsewhere. And so are his. Now is the time, they will say, when the lord displays his anger at the world. The sky which has been frail and

slow since dawn looks solid suddenly. It stiffens like a
muscle under stress. The air becomes so heavy that both
habitants and trespassers are made to duck their heads.
The wind is strong enough to make some of the marauders scuttle indoors and others to seek safety behind walls.
It strips the trees of their few remaining leaves and fruit
and slams all open doors. There is a distant cry, a fleshy
thundering, coming from the buildings at the garden's
heart. The lord is blustering, the few remaining brothers
and sisters say. Soon his fury will be physical. He will
reach down to save his eden from the world. But, as
quickly as it came, the wind eases and the sky softens,
just as a puffball softens when it's popped. It is as if the
universe of everything is now resigned to everlasting
change, without eternity. The air that everybody
breathes – whether they belong in there or not – is crisp
and fresh, less laden than it's ever been, less tart.

The incomers have filled their lungs. Their fear has
parted with the wind. Most are only boisterous and mean
no lasting harm. If some take hold of heavy knives from
the kitchens or the long-handled shovels that are used to
take the hot bread from the ovens or retrieve the scythes
the fleeing habitants have dropped, they are meant only
as trophies, reminders of this strange, exciting day. But
those few who are not boisterous are dangerous, especially when they see through the gaps and knot-holes of
the lofts a blue and bustling host of birds, enough to
stock a thousand feasts and put a stop to hunger, at least

257

until next autumn when hunger comes again with its first frost. They're not so very different now from the ravens – which, despite the snarling of the little dog but untroubled, though, by human kind – have shown up at Jamin's butchered carcass outside the hunter's hut. They're somewhat puzzled by the smell of fish but still jockey for position to better scavenge bloody residues and feast on innards, entrails, skin.

The latches on the timber doors are lifted by the bravest of the crowd and then they all rush in. Great shards of light stretch out across the floor. The first thing that they notice is the fluster and the smell, as if a dovecote has been broken into by a pack of cats. Whatever creatures have been kept inside this barn are in the rafters now and hardly visible, though the air is spiralling with dust. It must have seemed a good idea to throw some light into the lofts with flaming torches and lanthorns. But someone should have been more careful with the fire and not allowed a wisp of it to fall into the tinder of the hay-deep floor. It catches, crackles, flares and dances yellow-red. It soon becomes a raucous, overwhelming blaze. And then it seems as if the roofs have been thrown back and just as suddenly filled by fleeing birds, of a size and sort they've never seen before and will not ever see again.

Outside, the foragers and pillagers are bound to look up at the mayhem in the skies. What they witness is a sight to cherish and dismay. A great cloud of blue ascending plumes, a storm of feathers and a sea of smoke which emerge out of the skylights of the angels' lofts in harmonic unison. They rise and pale, then seem so small, it's said, that a hundred of them could easily find room enough to dance on the head of a pin. And then they disappear entirely into the thick and distant sky, to settle in their ancient places, never to return. Ebon thinks he must have seen the heavy, awkward flight of Jamin in the host and is glad of that. Tabi grips her brother by his elbow as the angels leave the world but does not look into the sky herself. It's better not to see. She's seen too much. Her head is heavy with experience. She does not know it yet, but in the time that she has left – in seed and fruit, in night and day, in famine and in feast – she will discover how to live and die in hope. As everybody must.

This is a story that will be told for years to come. A love story, a history, a tale of wisdom gained, of growing old, of treasuring what's drawn in air as much as what is solid earth and stone, of clinging close to flesh and bark, of birds and bells, of work and play, and forging out of hardship hope. This is a story that unends. But nobody who wasn't there to witness it will want to take it for the truth. Except, perhaps, if they are scrumping pears or apples during harvest and see a smiling face with great expanding eyes carved into the bark of a younger tree and ageing with the seasons. Or, indeed, if they could meet, before the spring returns with its green shoots – it will return, and then return, and then return again, time after time, until we are all out of time – a woman with a new-born child that's sporting on its head a bonnet brighter, bluer, than a summer sky and fashioned out of feathers from an angel's wing.